WHEN WE'RE HOME IN AFRICA

THEMBA UMBALISI

INTRODUCTION

My name is Themba Umbalisi. I did not know my great-great-great-grandfather, for he was dead some 40 years before I was born. I do not even know the name he had when he was born, or which he used in his young life. I did know the family stories, or legends, rather, for the tales were vague, as if people were talking about a ghost or a myth rather than a man of flesh, bone and blood.

Yet, when I found out more about my ancestor, I discovered that he was all flesh, bone, and blood, with a good dash of iron and guile into the bargain. Above all, he was a man with a man's virtues and weaknesses.

I considered myself as South African until the recent attacks on foreigners in Jo'burg and other parts of the country. That was five years ago in 2015. I was aware that I did not look quite like my neighbours, and I was neither wholly Zulu, Xhosa, nor any of the other peoples in this rainbow nation, but I was born and brought up in the country and lived here all my life. I was certainly not one of the Boers or others of European stock, yet the mob singled me out as not belonging and forced out of Jo'burg.

When the mob burned our house, very little survived of our

family possessions, except a chest that we used as a seat. I had seen it every day, but family tradition dictated that nobody should ever open it.

The mob threatened me with death unless I fled Jo'burg and South Africa, although I had no other place to call home and knew nothing except the rainbow country.

As I sat beside the road on the high veldt, with the flames of my burning home reflecting on the moody grey clouds, I kicked at the chest in frustration. It was a family tradition not to open that box, but I was the only member of the family present. Who would know? And in our current situation, who would care? Forcing open the ageing lock, I pushed up the lid, hoping to see treasures inside. I felt immediate disappointment, for there was very little.

I found a very tattered and much-repaired blue uniform jacket and a couple of faded sepia photographs of ancestors I did not recognize. There was also some battered Zulu clothing and what I thought was the remains of ostrich feathers and the rusted blade of an assegai. Finally, I saw an ancient pipe with a curved stem and an old British Martini-Henry rifle. I had hoped for something more useful, such as a bag of gold dust, but I contained my disappointment. Indeed, I was so sick at heart that I nearly missed the slim, leather-bound volume tucked into the bottom of the chest.

When I lifted it, I knew at once that the book held something important. I cannot explain the feeling; I can only say that I felt something surge through me, making all my nerve-ends tingle.

Sitting beside the road, with the memory of the mob fresh in my mind, I examined the book. The leather was rough like the hide of a buffalo, inexpertly tanned. The pages within were thin leather or thick parchment and uneven as if the writer had no access to any manufactured paper. Even the ink was unusual, faint in some places and dark in others. With nothing else to do and no hope for the future, I began to read what my distant ancestor had written.

I found the journal inspiring and will reread it whenever I feel down. I hope some of the readers do, too. I did not alter the journal much for publication. I merely tidied up some of the spelling and sent it to a publisher, with the result that you see here.

Themba Umbalisi

I AM FREED FROM SLAVERY AND
JOIN THE ARMY

I write this with a reed for a pen and a mixture of soot, ash and animal blood for ink. I have no paper, so I am using the dried hide of an impala instead. It has been many years since I last lifted a pen, or tried to communicate in English, so please excuse my mistakes in spelling or grammar.

I was born a slave and grew up on a plantation in Georgia. I don't remember much about my early years except constant fear and the whistle and crack of the whip. I will write what little I remember. We worked six days a week, from sunup to sundown, with an overseer or a slave driver, ensuring we did not stop working.

The overseer could be a white man, while the slave driver was black like ourselves. I remember my mother telling me that white slave owners were the devil's assistants and slave drivers were worse. We hated the drivers. I did not know my father because our owner gambled and lost him in a game of cards. I do not even remember how he looked. I loved my mother until the fever took her when I was young; I do not know how old I was. Perhaps I was ten, mebbe I was younger. For the same reason, I do not know how old I am now, so any ages within this journal

1

are only a guess. As nobody else knows or cares, my age does not matter much anyway.

We lived in fear of the whip and in fear of being sold. We lived in fear of the master and the slave driver. Most of all, we lived in fear of the mistress, who was a pretty blonde with a vicious temper. I remember her smile and the sudden curl of her lips as she ordered a slave, male or female, young or old, to be whipped.

Apart from that, I remember very little.

I do remember the day that freedom came. We heard the firing early in the morning and saw the smoke rising in the north and east. Our masters, as we called them, were mostly away in the war, and the few white men left on the plantation were either too old to fight or already disabled in battle. I saw all the white folk hurry away, and then the blue-uniformed soldiers marched in. They fed us, told us we were free and torched the plantation house.

I remember my first day of freedom. I sat, waiting to be fed, waiting for somebody to tell me what to do, waiting. The blue-coated soldiers had destroyed everything and then marched away, leaving a smoking ruin of the only home I had ever known, and I waited.

"What're you waiting on?" Emily, a slave like me and much older, asked.

"I'm waiting to see what happens now," I said.

"Ain't nothing going to happen now," Emily said, "less'n you make it. You're a free man."

"What do I do as a free man?" I asked.

"Whatever you want, boy," Emily said. "You're free to do anything you damned well want. That's what freedom means."

"I want to eat," I said, "but the blue soldiers burned the stores."

Emily cackled. "You wanted freedom," she said. "Now, you have it. Either earn some food or hunt it."

I stared at her without understanding. I was very young and

a lifetime on a plantation was not the best training for a life of freedom. Without any idea where I was going, I walked beyond the confines of the plantation and never looked back.

I don't know where I went or for how long I walked. I only remember walking through a scorched countryside, with smoking houses and broken fences, with the occasional dead bodies on the ground. I was always hungry and ate what I could scrape from fields, or find in the charred, deserted farmhouses.

"Hey, boy," a soldier in a blue coat said to me. "You want to eat?"

"Yes, sir," I said.

He tossed me the heel of a loaf. "Join the army, boy," he said. "Free food and clothes."

"Where can I join?" The offer of free food was too good to miss.

"Why, boy, right over there," he pointed to a tented camp.

And that is how I became a soldier.

"We don't want negro soldiers in the Union army," the sergeant was tall, red-faced and loud as she shouted in my face. He looked me up and down. "I suppose you might be useful to take a shot meant for a real soldier."

I said nothing to his insults. I only wanted to ensure that Lincoln's bluecoats won the war and I would be a free man. I wanted to end slavery forever. More than that, I wanted food.

"You see," the sergeant jabbed the end of his stubby pipe into my chest. "This war has got a deal of fighting in it yet, and the Rebs are a-going to kill a load of Union soldiers before we lick them."

I nodded, moving further away to avoid the painful prods from the sergeant's pipe.

"The way I see it," the sergeant said, following me up, "the more Negroes join our army, the fewer white men will die." He leaned back, thrust his pipe back in his mouth, quite satisfied with his logic. "After all, boy," he said, "it's your damned war we're fighting. It's about time you lifted your hands and did something for yourselves."

When he began to prod with his pipe again, I forgot that I was only a first-day recruit and he was a non-commissioned officer and therefore God's representative on Earth.

"Sergeant," I said slowly. "Has anybody ever hit you?"

He widened his eyes as if surprised at the idea. "Lordy, no!" he said. "Nobody would be that foolish." After that, he jabbed me again, harder, with that damned pipe until I took a swing at him.

I was big and strong and fast and missed completely. A sergeant in the Union Army did not achieve that rank without being able to fight. He dodged my punch without seeming effort and treated me, and all the other recruits, to a boxing lesson that had me floored in seconds.

"Up you get, Johnny Negro," he said. "I'll larn you to attack a superior."

And larn me he did. I did not give up. I rose and swung and punched and jabbed, and every time I missed, and he hit me with a fist like a steam hammer. Eventually, when I was a bloodied wreck on the ground, he stood over me with his pipe in his mouth, smiling.

"You damned foolish Negro," he said. "You'll never beat me. Get up." He landed a kick in my ribs.

I crawled to my feet, lifting my fists to fight again.

"You're a game one," the sergeant said. "Once we train you how to fight, you might even make a soldier. Now get back in the ranks."

The other recruits watched me as I limped painfully back into the ranks. I won't go into many details of that war of liberation. I was young, bewildered and often afraid, as I marched, counter-marched, camped and fought beside my fellow ex-slaves. I was one of the nearly 180,000 Negro soldiers that fought in the forces of freedom and marched for the glory of the lord. Even now I can sing every word of the "Battle Hymn of the Republic."

Mine eyes have seen the glory of the coming of the Lord
He is trampling out the vintage where the grapes of wrath are stored
He hath loosed the fateful lightning of His terrible swift sword
His truth is marching on; His truth is marching on.
Glory, glory, Hallelujah! Glory, glory, Hallelujah!
Glory, glory, Hallelujah! His truth is marching on.

I can see us now, the long columns marching with Old Glory at the head, the dust rising around us and the hopeful, eager black faces wearing the proud blue uniforms. And I can see the shattered, broken bodies lying in the mud and dirt, with blood soaking into the ground while powder-smoke bites into eyes and noses. I can see us sitting around camp-fires, weary under the lash of the rain, and preparing for battle, counting our ammunition, sharpening the long bayonets and praying the Lord spared us in the imminent carnage.

Glory glory.

About one-in-six of us died, and only God knows how many still carry the wounds on our bodies or inside our heads. Yet, we showed the slave owners that we could face them and outfight them on their own terms. We fought from Fort Wagner to Cold Harbour, Fort Pillow to the Crater at Petersburg.

Fort Pillow put a chill into our stomachs and iron in our hearts. The Confederates overran a Union garrison of mixed black and white soldiers and massacred the Negroes as they tried to surrender. I was not present there, but we heard the stories and swore vengeance if we ever got a slave-owner at the point of our bayonets. We hid our fear and marched on. Glory, glory hallelujah.

I was at the Crater, on the bloodiest day of my war and a battle I can still see in my nightmares. I have heard it tell that men become war-hardened, so that blood and death and slaughter do not bother them. That may be so, to a degree. Some men become insensitive to human suffering, and we learned to sleep on a battlefield with a comrade's corpse for a pillow as the wounded screamed around us. For most, however, the memories remained. At night, sixty years later, I relive the horrors and wake up with the fear of a Confederate bayonet snaking towards my guts, or the sound of the whimpering wounded in my ears.

Sometimes I relive that battle of the Crater. It was at the Crater that General Ambrose Burnside – the man after whom sideburns are named – sent me forward with General Edward Ferrero's Fourth Division of United States Colored Troops, as they called us. Federal forces had blown a mine under the Confederate positions, killing hundreds of Rebels and leaving a Crater and a gap in their defences. The original plan saw our Fourth Division attacking around the flanks of the Crater. Instead, the general sent a white unit forward, and they ran into the Crater. The Confederates recovered and mauled the white troops, and then we were sent in to rectify the position.

Burnside was a fool, one of the most inept commanders in an army not known for its tactical skills. In my opinion, the Union won that war by having massive manpower and resources, with few of the higher commanders fit for their positions. In that battle alone, hundreds of black soldiers fell.

All I recall of that day is the bank of white powder smoke, the constant flare of massed Confederate musketry and the hideous sound of the Rebel battle cry above the moans and cries of the wounded: that and the stubborn bravery of the black infantry.

From time to time, unrelated images emerge in my mind, usually at night as I wake from sleep, or struggle in the grip of some nightmare that soaks my coverings with sweat. My wives come to wake me, then, and I remember that the past is gone and can't return. Yet still, I remember the man with only half a head and his brains seeping out, the soldier staring as his intestines slithered from his body, and the young boy begging me to end his agony by killing him.

I did, God forgive me. I shot my comrade in the head and killed him dead.

When the general ordered the retire, many of us refused to

run from the men who had held us as slaves, and the Confederates shot us down like rabbits. I was one of the casualties. When the battle ended, I lay on the battlefield with two Confederate balls in me, one in the shoulder and one in my left leg.

I lay there for hours, bothered by questing flies until a black corporal and a white private carried me to a field hospital. If a battlefield is hell on earth, a field hospital is the devil's playground. It is a place of pain, suffering, death and disease, of amputated limbs and screaming wounded, of callous medical orderlies and brave men howling, of sickening wounds and buzzing flies. If anybody ever thinks that war is glorious, let him work in a field hospital for one night, and I defy him to ever don a uniform of whatever hue or colour. Politicians who wish to start a war should be forced to work in there for a week, just one week, to let them see the horrors their decisions inflict on men.

I returned to duty five months later, but without seeing any more significant action in that war. I did have the satisfaction of being involved in liberating some plantations. In one, I chopped down the whipping post and wanted to tie up a slave driver we captured, to see how he felt on the receiving end. Our lieutenant, a young man from Vermont, seemed quite taken with the idea, but the captain would not hear of it. The slave driver escaped, although I heard that an ex-slave woman found him a year later and shot him dead. I hope that is true.

After all the blood and bravery, after all the dust had settled, after we helped the Union crush the proud Confederacy, what did we gain? Ten dollars a month, a third less than the white soldiers. And we got the Ku Klux Klan, a measure of false freedom, and the sinking feeling of despair that we would never be equal in the United States of America.

"You'll have to learn to walk before you can run," the sergeant of a white New York regiment said to me.

I did not believe him. I thought we had won our freedom. I did not know how deep the white man's prejudice sank beneath his colourless skin. We marched and fought for a freedom we thought we had gained.

Peace brought disbandment, and, for me, disillusionment. I found the reality of freedom did not meet my expectations.

In theory, all black slaves in the United States were free. In practice, we had to work to earn money to eat, and the only work I could do was plantation work or soldiering. As I hungered, new state laws reintroduced slavery in all but name. After the war, the army quickly disbanded its black regiments, and I refused to work on a plantation again, slave or free. As a consequence, I drifted for a while. I picked up a little labouring work here and there, thought of heading west to the Frontier and contemplated becoming an outlaw or a gold prospector.

I was wandering one day, with my head down and my uniform tattered, faded and dusty, when I heard a voice calling to me.

"Soldier!"

I looked up to see a white woman at the side of the road. I'd reckon she was thirty, so at least ten years older than me, not ill-favoured but worn down with hardship. "You looking for work?"

"Yes, ma'am," I said.

"Winter's coming on," she said bluntly. "I need a man to keep my cabin waterproof, do the labouring, that sort of thing. No wages, but food and board. You'd sleep in the barn."

"I've slept in worse," I said, following her.

The woman was the widow of a soldier, a corporal who had died at Bull Run, and she treated me well. "Folks will wonder at me for giving work to a Negro," she told me openly. "Well, as I see it, you're a soldier boy like my Tom was, and that's an end to it."

I worked that winter and stayed with the widow-woman, a Mrs Ebenezer Wilson. I learned a lot those four months. I learned how to ride a horse. I learned that a poor white woman was not too proud to accept help from a poor black man, and I learned that by standing together, they could face poverty better than they could alone.

We shared many things that winter of 1865 and early spring of 1866, including Mary's bed. It was a rough night, I recall, with the rain lashing at the wooden barn like an overseer's whip, and the wind whistling through the boards like the devil calling up the demons of hell. I lay there on the straw with an old horse blanket over me and a saddle for a pillow when I became aware of Mrs Wilson standing in the doorway. She was looking at me.

"You'll be cold," she said, a statement rather than a question.

"I am," I agreed.

"It's warmer in the house," she said, turned and walked away.

I followed and stepped into the two-room shack, where a small fire sparked in the stone fireplace and food sat in bowls on the table.

"Eb made that table," Mrs Wilson said. "He cut the trees, sawed the planks and made the table. He made the chairs too, and built the house."

I nodded, unsure what to say.

"We had the place looking fit, and the damned war came along."

I nodded again. I had thought the war a good thing, for freeing us slaves, but it had not been good for Mrs Wilson, or tens of thousands of women like her.

"Damned useless war," Mrs Wilson glared at me, as if challenging me to argue.

I was sensible enough to keep my peace and enjoy the warmth of the fire.

"Your clothes are wet," Mrs Wilson said. "Take them off."

She watched as I obeyed, nodding. "I haven't known a man since Ebenezer died," she said.

I nodded again, feeling her eyes scrutinizing me.

"You'll do," she said. "Come on."

Mrs Wilson was not the first woman I had known, but the

others had been whores, women of the street, the riff-raff who follow every army. Mrs Wilson was not of that type, she needed the comfort of a man's body as I needed the comfort of a woman's, and it was with regret that I said farewell. It was the summer of 1866, and the road was calling. I liked the woman, but not sufficient to remain with her, with the inevitable trouble such a union would bring to us both. Except on the wildest of frontiers, the world does not smile on a black man with a white woman. I did not wish to survive slavery and the war to die at the end of a lynching rope. As the buds turned to leaves and the birds greeted summer with elaborate mating calls, I took the highway northward and did not look back.

In the high summer of 1866, Congress realised the mistake they had made in disbanding the black regiments. After deliberation, they authorised six Negro regiments to fight for the reunited United States. I did not see myself as an itinerant labourer, working for white folk for the rest of my life, and at least in the army, I was with my own kind, doing work I understood. A man feels proud when he carries a gun, and a black man had little chance to bear arms in 1866. I was no lover of the South and thought they owed me for past suffering, so stealing a horse did not disturb my conscience. After years of slavery and fighting with the Union army, I had little conscience to disturb. I had enough of marching in the Civil War, so I looked for a recruiting station and put myself forward for the cavalry. I headed south again and rode to the headquarters of the 9th Cavalry at Greenville, Louisiana.

I BECOME A CAVALRY TROOPER

"**Y**ou've been in the army," the recruiting sergeant, a one-armed man with deep brown eyes, viewed the remnants of my uniform.

"Yes, Sergeant," I said.

"Infantry," he told me.

"Yes, Sergeant."

"Can you ride a horse?"

"Yes, Sergeant." I knew the military style: answer directly, don't waste words. I did not mention the horse tethered outside the building.

"Did you see any action?"

I gave the sergeant a resume of my military career.

"The Crater, eh?" He nodded. "That's good enough for me. Welcome to the 9th Cavalry." And that was me back in the Army again as a black man in a blue uniform defending white men from red men. In common with the other recruits, I had signed my life away for the next five years. At my young age, five years seemed an eternity.

There were two black cavalry regiments, the 9th and the 10th. My name is on the muster roll of the 9th, somewhere, I imagine, or the name I called myself then. I used a false name, for I did not want to be Solomon Blackman any longer.

The 9th Cavalry was a strange formation, with white officers and a full-time dedicated chaplain. The chaplain's primary function was to care for our souls as we trained to be effective killers, but he had a secondary task in educating his flock in reading, writing and arithmetic. He was an intense, likeable man who did his best with a difficult set of pupils, and he taught me a lot.

Colonel Hatch commanded us, and a man more opposite to his troopers it is hard to imagine. A blonde sailor from Maine, he had fought through the war from 1861 to its close, by which time he was a brevet Major-General. It was not long after I joined the unit that I learned that a certain George Custer had refused the command of our regiment because we were black, and therefore not good enough for him. Well, after a few weeks under Colonel Hatch, I can say we got the best of the bargain, and our colonel commanded a better regiment than the 7th ever was. Custer was a man who liked to tell the world how good he was and led his men to disaster in the pursuit of personal glory. The Sioux later reproved his arrogance, I believe.

Colonel Hatch had no difficulty in raising the troopers for the 9th, but experienced problems finding officers. Black men were not permitted to become officers, and most white men did not wish to serve with coloured troops. They thought they were better than us. Having seen some of the drunkards and stupid officers during the war, I cannot agree. I think they were lucky to have us.

There are two sides to every coin. I was not impressed by many of the troopers the Army recruited into the 9th. As I watched them come into the barracks, I could see they were not joining because of any desire for military service, but for the 13-dollars-a-month pay, plus food and a place to stay. Many were local, from Louisiana, others from Kentucky and other states. One man who I became friendly with was a Kentuckian named

William Sharpe. He was a fellow labourer with a ready smile and a laugh that could charm the angels from Heaven. Everybody liked William.

"Here we are then," William said on his very first day as he bounced on the straw mattress. "A free house, free food, free clothes, something to pass the day and the Army even pay us!" He grinned across to me. "Who'd be anything other than a soldier?"

I laughed, guessing there were hard days ahead. "Is this the life you dreamed of?"

"Why, no, sir," William said. "I'm only passing the time until better fortune favours me and then I'm going home to Africa!"

I got used to that phrase, for when things were bad, William always gave us his broadest smile. "Never care, gentlemen in blue," he would say, "someday we'll be home in Africa."

Someday we'll be home in Africa. I held onto those words through the dark times, for they lit a flame within me. Until I met William, I had never even dreamed of Africa, or of a home. I had no conception of such an idea. I never thought of the plantation as home, while the Army was a refuge from the outside world, nothing more. I suppose. If anything, I had felt more at home with Mrs Wilson than anywhere else, although I had never considered that house as anything more than temporary.

We bunked together, William and I, and were to fight back to back in skirmishes along the bloody frontier in years to come. At that time, I did not know how close we were to become, and only enjoyed his caustic humour, his ready acceptance of hardship and danger and his friendship. In my earlier Army experience, I had known comradeship; with William Sharpe, it was more profound. I have heard that man and man can share a love deeper than any we know with women, and with William, I believe that was true. We understood each other better than man and woman can ever do and shared the same dangers and interests. Oh, there was never any sexual desire and nothing unnatural between us. We were like brothers and William made the 9th Cavalry bearable.

I found myself a veteran amongst a set of greenhorns. All the troopers had been born to slavery, and none of us was used to the responsibilities of freedom. The chaplain did his best to educate and advise, but he was a lone voice in the wilderness of babble. Most of the men were very young, some unfit or plainly unwell, unused to self-discipline and not inclined to listen to anybody who spoke sense. At first, William was as bad as the worst of them, and I fear that at times I was not much better. We acted likes babes with drink, like unregulated youths with women, and like fools with gambling and money. Fights were frequent, fists and boots flashing, and we were not the best examples of young manhood. White officers were slow to arrive, our NCOs were inexperienced and lacked authority, and left to our own devices, young men seldom decide to hold church services and polish their piety.

That camp was as near to hell as anywhere outside a slave plantation or a Confederate prison camp. Young men gambled away all they had, even to the very clothes on their back, so a few recruits huddled in complete nudity. The whores who infested the camp loved that and tormented the naked boys with barbed words and coarse comparisons. These hell-women added their noxious diseases to the expected horrors of dysentery and fever that haunt any crowded camp. And Greenville was crowded.

We lived in cotton compresses, cooked inadequate food over smoky fires of damp wood, drank to excess and fought over insults fancied or real. The whores fought and swore as much as the men, scratching, biting, gouging and kicking to settle their differences, with the officers turning a blind eye and the NCOs chasing their tails and achieving nothing.

William took up with a harlot, leaving me alone with only the bottle and gloomy thoughts for company. I began to get morose and contemplated desertion until winter cholera claimed

William's whore and I remained with the 9th. After all, where else could I go? I was a soldier, I decided, nothing else. Soldiering was my destiny until I could get to Africa. I smiled bitterly into the bottom of my glass, swirled the moonshine whiskey and laughed at my pretensions. How the hell could I ever get to Africa when I didn't even know where it was? I looked up as the padre entered the room.

"Here, padre!" I shouted across to him. "Where's Africa?"

He came across to me, ignoring the antics of a near-naked harlot who sought to shock him. "Come with me, and I'll show you on a map."

That day I learned where Africa was, and where my ancestors might have come from, and knew I would like to visit, someday, somehow. I did not know how.

After a brutal winter, when only a dozen officers trickled into the 9th, we heard that the Federal government was sending us to the western frontier.

As a soldier, I expected nothing less. The Army was there to fight, and the enemy was whoever the President decided. I had no compunction about fighting anybody, of any race, colour or creed. Fighting was my job. Other men did not see things my way, and some of the recruits muttered their discontent. I knew we were not ready to fight, being half-trained at best, and we were undoubtedly unfit to face any Indian tribe. However, I did not make the decision.

At that time, I was in Company K, and we rode from Louisiana to San Antonio in Texas. I found that marching with the Union Army during the Civil War and marching with a half-trained mob of not-yet soldiers were two different things. During the war, we had a purpose, a cause in which we all believed. Now, the greenhorns complained about everything. They wanted the wages and the uniforms but rebelled against the hardships. Many were too young, too weak and too stupid to be horse soldiers of the Republic. I was not surprised when the 9th

struggled on the road, and half expected the mutiny that broke out in Company K.

I do not know who started the trouble. I was with William at the time, riding in columns of two, deep in the Texas brushland, when we heard the shouting. The NCOs tried their best but did not have the experience to control a rioting mob, which is what K Company had become. With so few officers, it took a while to regain control of the company, and to this day, I do not know what sparked the outbreak. I do know that it left a bad feeling behind it, and the troopers marched into San Antonio in a sullen mood, looking for trouble.

Trouble, in the Texas of the 1860s, was not hard to find. Neither the citizens nor the police of San Antonio welcomed us, for two reasons. The first reason was that we wore the hated blue uniforms of the Union and the second was that we were black.

I cannot recall the number of incidents between the 9th Cavalry and the Texans, but they were many, and our men were eager to retaliate. Sometimes we even retaliated first, and discontent simmered under our government blue. Why were we defending these men – and women – who openly despised us?

There was another mutiny, and a more serious one, in April, with K Company again to the fore. This time A and E Companies joined in. William had heard the whispers of anger and warned me, so we knew to avoid the flashpoints. I was torn between warning the colonel and joining in but decided to remain quiet and allow matters to take their course. I could not betray my fellows, young fools though they were, but neither could I side with white men against black. The memories of slavery were still too strong, and the 9th Cavalry had not yet combined into a unified regiment.

As I remember, Lieutenant Griffin of A Company died, along with two troopers of my K Company. Griffin was unpopular and a bully. We did not miss him. I knew one of the troopers, although I cannot remember his name, only his face. Memory is like that, some things are imprinted on one's mind, indelibly, as if they happened only yesterday, and others are faded, like old pictures, hazy memories of long-gone people, ghosts that can never return.

Colonel Hatch and the government responded by increasing the number of officers in the 9th. If they had acted with such decision during the winter, there would have been no mutiny, and three men would have been alive to face the country's enemies. As it was, no sooner had the new officers arrived than we were on the march.

"Saddle up, boys," our lieutenant ordered, with a smile on his face but his hand close to his sword in case we refused the order. Mutiny casts a long, dark shadow.

"Where are we going, sir?" William asked.

"Westward," the lieutenant said, without moving his hand. "Westward to the frontier. We're going to earn our wages."

I decided that a cheer might help, so yelled out, with William not far behind me. Others joined in, as we tried to show that Company K had put its past behind it and was ready to face the future, whatever that held. The lieutenant visibly relaxed when we obeyed his order and mounted our horses. Company K, the 9th US Cavalry, was riding to war.

We headed westward, hundreds of untried black soldiers riding to guard an untamed frontier that stretched hundreds of miles. As we rode, the news filtered down from above. We were to garrison Fort Davis and Fort Stockton, which were only names to me. I know nothing about these places, and at that time, cared less. I was a soldier, I had a job to do, and that was sufficient.

At that time, the ordinary troopers carried the Spencer repeating carbine, with the NCOs having a revolver. The revolver was the Colt Army 44, single action, six shots, and proven in the late war, as long as one was close to the enemy and did not expect accuracy. The Spencer was a large 56.50 calibre weapon with a seven-shot magazine. I believe it was the only magazine carbine in existence at the time, and superior to the rifles other armies used. To load, we simply pushed the magazine into the stock through a slot in the butt plate. There was a flaw because the cartridges were in a row, so sometimes the Spencer fired itself, hitting anybody foolish, or unfortunate, enough to be in line with the muzzle.

I saw more than one trooper of the 9th fall that way, even before we faced the Comanche or the Apache. Later, I think it was 1873, the Army issued us with the much superior Springfield.

Although we did not know it, the 9th Cavalry was destined to remain on the Rio Grande frontier for years. Indeed, I spent the remainder of my time with the 9th in Texas. While the 10th Cavalry had the glory of facing the Southern Plains Indians, the Kiowa-Apaches, Kiowa, Comanches and southern Cheyanne, we had less glamour but equal, or more, danger.

"Well, boys," the colonel addressed Company K, "we're bound for some hard days ahead, guarding the frontier." He looked at us, assessing our abilities. "We can," he said, "and we will."

We nodded at this expression of trust, and I noted his inclusiveness. He did not mention our colour or the mutiny; he called us 'we,' and that meant a lot. We were together in this. We were all soldiers in blue uniforms; we were the 9th Cavalry.

As I listened to the colonel, I looked at my fellow soldiers. Most were very young, barely shaving, with no idea of warfare. Some were eager to prove themselves, others plainly nervous. Many, perhaps the majority, wished to identify with the white officers, to prove themselves worthy of fighting alongside the white man. I may have shared that view to an extent, for I knew that the white man thought of us as inferior. That was a legacy of slavery. It was a legacy I did not wish to retain.

"The United States depends on you, boys," the colonel said, with the wind catching his hat and his eyes the brightest blue. "We're all that stands between civilisation and the wild redmen of the Kickapoos and Lipans, the Mexicans and outlaws." He paused. "And the Apaches."

I heard that last word with a sinking sensation inside my stomach. All the red men were dangerous; each Indian tribe had its warriors who would kill a black man or a white man with equal relish. However, the Apache had a certain notoriety for savagery and cruelty that surpassed all the others.

"I would not like to meet the Apaches," I said.

"Nor would I," William told me.

"If they capture me," I said, "shoot me, William. Don't let the red devils torture me."

William nodded. "You do the same for me."

We shook hands on our private arrangement.

"Someday we'll be home in Africa," William said, stuffing tobacco in his pipe. William was proud of his pipe, a huge, hand-made thing he told me his father had carved.

I laughed, without taking him seriously, for fear of the Apaches dominated my thoughts. William was the only trooper I knew who spoke of sailing to Africa.

"The Federal Government have a settlement there," he told me one night. "It's called Liberia, and any ex-slaves can go there. Once I leave the Army, I'm going home to Africa."

I listened without much hope. I had lived all my life in the United States, as had my parents. I did not know beyond that, for my family history was lost. I thought of Africa as a barbarous place, far away from our American civilisation. It was far beyond my expectations, yet William spoke of it as his homeland, as if he had a right to be there.

The day before we headed for the frontier, I became involved in a fistfight. I was outside the fort on my own when a couple of white citizens took exception to me. They might have objected to my blue uniform or my black skin, I did not know, and nor did I care. I was happy to take them on, for I was now a veteran of many barrack-room brawls and inter-regimental battles. I could hold my own in any fistfight and fancied I could whip a brace of cougars, let alone two ranting Texans.

By that time, we wore our drinking jewellery whenever we ventured outside the security of the battalion. That was what we called our fighting rings, horseshoe nails bent around each finger, with the head thrust up to tear and rip the skin of our opponent. With that aid, plus my natural aggression, I was well on top when more Texans joined up. One hit me on the back of the head, and another grabbed my arms, pinning me as the others landed swinging punches to my stomach.

I was kicking out, losing the fight when William turned up to help. The Texans did not expect us to support each other. We stood back to back and fought them off with boots and fists, two black men against I don't know how many white. I have little recollection of what happened except seeing a mass of white faces, bearded or unshaven, with open pink mouths and blind, unreasoning hatred in their eyes.

Why did they hate us? What had we ever done to them?

Our ancestors did not ask them to carry us to America as slaves. We did not force them to make us toil for their profit, or demand that they place us in shackles, or whip us until we fainted through loss of blood. Now we were in their army, defending their frontier against Indians, the people they displaced to steal their lands. Why did the white men hate us? Was it an expression of their guilt? Did they hate us because we reminded them of their sins? Or did they hate us merely because we were black?

I do not know, and I did not think any of these things when the screaming white mob surrounded us.

The arrival of a corporal and three men of Company K altered the situation. The mob melted away, as mobs do when confronted by resistance, and there the incident ended. Or nearly, for the regiment did not approve of fighting and sentenced William and me to stand on the edge of a barrel for six hours.

William looked at me as we balanced in the hot sun and grinned. "It will be better when we're home in Africa," he said.

I held on to his words, and we used them as a mantra whenever things were grim. Home in Africa became our dream, an impossibly bright future that we hoped for in some unimaginable happy time to come. If only we could survive the next day, the next week, the next five years.

Garrison life on the frontier began in the usual army fashion. We formed work details for building barracks, stables and corrals for the horses until we all became experts with axes, saws and shovels.

"If I wanted to be a labourer, I'd have remained at home," Will said.

"Keep quiet and keep sweating, trooper!" Sergeant Bell shouted. "You're here to work, not to grumble!"

We worked, watching the fort grow by the labour of our backs and the sweat of our brows. More beasts of burden than troopers of the Republic, we worked with our Spencers close to hand, for nobody knew when the Indians might raid.

Slowly, day by day, Company K and the 9th Cavalry became a cohesive unit. We trained with the horses, and on foot, we trained with the carbines, loading, aiming and firing, aware that the next time we fired, it might be at a live Indian intent of scalping us. That knowledge put an edge that our training had lacked in Louisiana. In every spare minute, unless I was with William, I sought the chaplain and asked him to teach me how to read and write. At that time, I thought that education was my key to advancement. If I proved myself the equal to the white men, I hoped, they would accept me. Once I learned the basics of reading and writing, the chaplain introduced me to books. It is hard to read in a crowded barrack-room when surrounded by young men with no interest in education. I persevered, and when the hazing became too severe, William would step in. Together, our fists and boots made space, and I continued my book learning.

In January 1867, the Comanches, always a volatile tribe, became active. We heard rumours about small parties of the younger warriors dancing the war dance, tales of men painting their faces and of the Comancheros, the despised gun-and-whiskey-smugglers visiting the reservation. All the same, it was a shock when the Comanches' war parties broke out. The braves attacked frontiersmen, settlers and railroad surveying parties, killing, mutilating and scalping all they could. We of the 9th checked our carbines, groomed our horses and awaited the order to ride out.

Meanwhile, General Sherman arrived in San Antonio in person, then rode to the frontier with an escort of the 10th Cavalry. We were unhappy at not being included and made our feelings known. Despite Sherman's presence, the Comanche raids continued. Seeing their example, the Kiowas also broke out. We waited, seething, for the order to ride. We were fit, we were ready, and we were the 9th Cavalry. All we wanted was the chance to prove our worth.

Spring and summer were the worst times for Indian trouble. Then the tribes had grass for their horses, the young brave's blood was coursing and the weather best for riding. We waited, practised our marksmanship and hoped to escape the tedium of garrison life.

I AM A BUFFALO SOLDIER

*A*round this time, or perhaps later, I heard the name the Indian tribes termed the 10th Cavalry. The 10th was on the Prairies by then, making a name for themselves against the redmen, who called them Buffalo Soldiers. We heard many stories about the origin of the term, without any evidence of truth, but we thought that Buffalo Soldiers was a term of respect. Gradually, year by year, we of the 9th adopted the name, and we also became Buffalo Soldiers. It was a name I was to use all my life.

The 9th was based in West Texas and along the Rio Grande, which formed part of the border between the United States and Mexico. Nobody needed to tell the troopers of the 9th that we guarded one of the most dangerous frontiers of the American West, and one of the most volatile in the world.

"Well," William said, lighting his pipe, "we're going to war."

"We are," I agreed. "Remember our agreement, William. We won't let the Apaches take us alive."

William nodded solemnly. "We'll make memories to bore our grandchildren when we're home in Africa." He blew a cloud of blue smoke into the air.

I laughed, although my spirits were not high. I did not share the enthusiasm of the younger troopers, who boasted of the great deeds they would do. I had seen the reality of war, and there was no glory. There was only agony, suffering and sordid, undignified death. Nobody died well in battle. "God help us all," I said.

After all this time, my memory of precise dates, names and events can be vague, so forgive me for any errors. I am sure somebody will write a history of the 9th Cavalry sometime, to add martial glory to what was a thankless, dirty job of small patrols and bloody skirmishes on the borderlands. My story is only personal memoirs, what I saw, heard and experienced in my life. I cannot and will not try to create a full historical picture of every event.

In the summer of 1867, we garrisoned Fort Stockton and Fort Davis. Stockton was a large place, and when we finished building, it had limestone and timber buildings rising from the flat Texas plain. Our orders were to prevent the Indians from attacking the stagecoaches on the road between El Paso and San Antonio, ensure the mail reached its destination and keep the peace. For a single raw, half-trained regiment, it was a near impossibility.

I had already marched and fought through much of the southeastern United States; now I patrolled in what we called brush jungle beside the Rio Grande, and over the deserts and plains of Texas. For the next few years, the 9th suffered from poor quality mounts and a lack of ammunition, as did other US cavalry regiments all across the West. Some of our horses had seen service in the Civil War, old, worn-out brutes that could hardly raise a canter, let alone a gallop. The US government got their soldiers on the cheap and expected miracles. We of the 9th did what the white regiments did, no worse, and possibly a little better. Does every unit not think it is the best?

We worked in bad country of extreme temperatures and wild men, usually in small patrol groups, with miles of hostile terrain separating us from support. Looking back, when I have fought and campaigned in two continents, and have fought professional soldiers of the Confederacy and the redcoats of the British Army as well as tribesmen in Africa and Texas, I count myself as something of an expert. I can say that the Mescalero Apaches were maybe the best irregular warriors I ever faced. However, we had many other enemies in old Texas. Where the Apaches raided from the Guadalupe Mountains, the Comanche and Kiowa could break from their reservations and plunder at will.

At that time I was stationed at Fort Stockton at Comanche Springs, right across the Comanche war trail. We earned our dollars in routine patrolling as well as escort duties and the occasional skirmish with Apache or Comanche war parties. Compared with the slaughter of the Civil War, it was small-scale soldiering, with less possibility of death or dismemberment, but the combat was real when it came, and the danger as intense. A Comanche arrow could kill as effectively as a Rebel bullet, and our daily dread was the fear of capture. We all knew what the Indians did to their captives. That was a topic of conversation in Stockton when some of us openly voiced our fears, and others pretended we were not scared. I noticed that William smoked more, furiously puffing at his long-stemmed pipe, and distracted him with games of cards and dice.

We were inseparable, William and I, guarding each other's backs on patrol and in barracks, ensuring we were fit for parade and war. When we could, we spent our money on the harlots that somehow drifted this far west, plump little Indian squaws, hard-eyed white women with knowing eyes, and the Mexicans with volatile tempers. I can see William yet, as we bounced around side by side, each with our woman, releasing the tension of a long patrol. I can see his smile and smell the smoke of his pipe.

During this period, I followed orders, did my duty, kept my head down and perfected my tasks as a cavalry trooper. As an infantryman, I had learned to cope with blisters and fatigue in my legs. As a cavalryman, the aches and pains were equally real, except in different parts of the body. We hardened up, in more ways than one.

During these early months, I faced hostile Indians, Mexican bandits, American cattle rustlers and the Comancheros. The Comancheros we despised as they ran rot-gut firewater whiskey and Spencer rifles to the Indians, and anybody else who could pay with stolen horses or cattle. The Comanches got drunk on the whiskey and used the Spencers to murder settlers and cavalry troopers, by which time the Comancheros were long gone. We took particular satisfaction in rounding up Comancheros and handing them in to the civilian authorities.

The work details were long, hard and punishing. When we arrived, Fort Stockton was a mess. When not on patrol, I spent my time cutting logs and general labouring, with Sergeant Greaves taking a dislike to me.

"You were an infantryman," he said, pushing his broad face against mine.

"Yes, Sergeant," I said.

"You fought in the War," he said, with his smoky, bloodshot eyes never straying from mine.

"Yes, Sergeant," I said.

"You think that makes you better than us," Sergeant Greaves decided and raised the tone of his voice to a bellow. "I don't agree!"

For the next hour, Greaves made me march around the fort, saluting every officer I met and telling every NCO that I thought I was better than him. Most of the NCOs recognised I was being hazed and refused to react. One or two of the recently promoted corporals gave me a buffet or extra duties, which amused Greaves a great deal.

That day was only the start. Every time I was free in the fort, Greaves would seek me out, yell at me or put me on punishment detail, such as standing on the end of a barrel for hours at a time in the unrelenting sun. It was unpleasant, yet I knew that Greaves could only torment me to a limited extent. I would survive. I vowed that, if ever the Apaches captured Greaves, I would not intervene. Twice, William brought me water when I was on the barrel, which earned him a few hours at my side.

I remember some of the young men complaining about the food, but although it was monotonous, it was adequate. Bread, beans, beef and coffee, and it was better than anything in the old plantation days. I compared that to my civilian days when I wandered without shelter or food. The 9th Cavalry seemed like paradise when I looked back. I set my jaw, endured Sergeant Greaves's torments and did my duty.

Some incidents stick in my mind. Not long after we arrived in West Texas, I was on duty protecting a herd of cattle from raiding Indians – Comanches, if I recall correctly. It was a long, tedious ride in the dust and I was glad to return to the fort. Unfortunately, Sergeant Greaves had other ideas and detailed me to a scouting detachment on the Pecos River.

"You can show us all how good you are," Greaves said, sneering.

"Yes, Sergeant," I said, and remounted my horse.

"No," Colonel Hatch had been listening. "You've done your duty, trooper. The sergeant will find another man."

It was a small incident, but after that day, Greaves hated me more than ever.

This soldiering was vastly different from the old Civil War days. There were no battles, only small-scale skirmishes and long dusty patrols, mainly on and around the road between El Paso and San Antonio. When the Indians struck, they were fast and often deadly, killing and scalping civilians and small parties of Buffalo Soldiers whenever they could. Usually, we arrived too late, only finding the mutilated bodies of the dead, or chasing shadows as the Mescaleros vanished into the vastness of Texas. We relished any skirmishes as it broke the frustration and gave us a chance to fight the most elusive enemy I have ever known.

I was on patrol, I think it was December 1867, when upwards of a hundred Mescalero Apaches ambushed the stage from El

Paso to San Antonio. We heard the firing from two miles away and rode to the rescue.

Until that minute, my service as a Buffalo Soldier had been routine. I had laboured, marched, patrolled and stood guard with barely a sign of a hostile. I had always been too far away to take part, and although I had seen Indians in the distance, I had not fired a single shot at them. I was a virgin Indian fighter. That mad ride along the San Antonio road, with the dust rising all around, our hats flying free, and us giving the horses their heads under the bright Texas sun lives with me still. We whooped like Johnny Reb infantry and started firing as soon as we saw the Mescaleros.

Now, whatever people say, a man on a galloping horse cannot fire accurately with a rifle. He can fire into a mass of enemy and hope to score a hit, but it would take an exceptional shot to hit a specific target. We intended only to scare the Mescaleros away and notify the stage of our presence.

The Mescaleros vastly outnumbered us and seemed inclined to fight. Rather than run, as was their usual practise when the 9th approached, they faced us. The driver of the stagecoach whipped like a hero, holding the reins one-handed while the guard fired and loaded as the arrows flew. I saw at least one arrow thud into the body of the coach and thrum there, an ugly growth on the woodwork.

We fired, loaded and fired, replied to the war-whoops of the Apache with shouts of our own and tried to form a screen around the beleaguered coach.

"We are the 9th Cavalry!" William roared.

And we were. We were the 9th Cavalry doing the job we were paid to do, defending the frontier from the red barbarians. Except there were very few of us compared to the enemy.

The Mescaleros circled and charged, and we rode hard, firing and loading, trying to avoid the flying arrows and the bullets. I saw Nathan Johnson fall, the first casualty of the 9th that I had known personally. The Apache, a basic tribal people, killed him despite his uniform and modern carbine. One minute he was alive, and the next he was on the ground with one foot in the stirrups and his head trailing in the dust. I did not know which warrior killed Nathan and had seen sufficient death not to be upset. William, however, was new to this side of soldiering. He rode straight for the Apaches, intent on revenge. I spurred after him, shouting and choking in the rising dust.

"William!" I shouted. "Come back!"

William was firing like a madman, holding his carbine one-handed as the Apaches formed an avenue in front of him. I knew that trick; the Apaches would pretend to flee, then close ranks and trap William in the middle, stun him and take him away for torture, scalping and death.

"William!" Rather than attack the Apaches, I rode alongside William, grabbed hold of his reins and pulled him away. I think the language I used must have shocked him back to his senses, for he followed me like a lamb, and we resumed our places in the screen. Fortunately, the confusion of battle prevented any officer from witnessing our acts, or we would both have been in trouble on our return.

They were persistent, these Apaches, and harassed us along that road until Captain Henry Carroll brought up Company F from Eagle Springs Station. The sound of the cavalry bugle was one of the sweetest I had heard for months. We heard the shrill notes from a quarter of a mile away and looked up through our sweat-stinging eyes to see the cloud of dust that heralded Company F.

The sun reflected on bridles and the metal of carbines, and then we saw the guidon raised high, the swallow-tail flag that told us we were no longer alone. Still, the Apache did not flee, firing a last salvo of arrows and bullets, and not until Company F was within three hundred yards did the Indians break off their attack.

"Thank you," William said to me.

I shook my head, for I was not used to accepting thanks. We

rode back to the fort, side by side, with our friendship now cemented in battle. William took out his curved pipe and stuffed tobacco in the bowl, looking at me from the corner of his eyes, as if in disbelief. We never mentioned that incident again. We were comrades and friends, and that was all that mattered.

"When we're in Africa," William said that night as we lay in our beds, "we'll look back at these days and laugh. What stories we will tell our grandchildren!"

"What's Africa like?" I asked.

"It's big and green and hot," William said. "My mother used to tell me about it. She says the people live in villages and the women do most of the work. All the men do is hunt, loaf in the sun, make babies and sometimes fight."

I laughed. "That sounds like the ideal life."

"There are huge kingdoms in Africa," William said. "Dahomey, Asanti, Sokoto, Bornu and others, all ruled by black men like us. Imagine having a black country with a black ruler."

I listened to him, trying to imagine a place where black people ruled. "I'd like to go there someday."

"We will," William told me. "You and I. Once we've finished our time in the Army, we'll go to Africa, find a black kingdom and join their army. They'll welcome us as veteran soldiers."

I had never heard such dreams before. I listened in awe. "How can we get there?"

"The federal government helps black people get back to Africa," William said. "They've got a country for black Americans. We can go there, then head for one of the black kingdoms."

I could have hugged myself in delight at the thought. I lay awake, dreaming of being a soldier, an officer perhaps, in a black army fighting for a black kingdom. William was like that; he could give ideas and make you think things you had never considered before. That was one reason why everybody liked him.

After that encounter with the Apaches, morale in the fort was high, but I hoped for a respite. Instead, the colonel sent William and me back to Company K, over 70 miles east of Fort Stockton, at Fort Lancaster. This fort is in Live Oak Creek, where the road between El Paso and San Antonio crosses the Pecos River. Unlike Stockton, Lancaster is – or was - nearly all military, with only a stage stop for any civilians; it was also one of the most remote posts in all of Texas. William told me the Union had established Lancaster back in 1855, but abandoned in 1861 with the war. When the soldiers marched away, the fabric crumbled, so we used the site as a base, camping in the open until we built it up again, stone by stone and log by log. Naturally, the Army did not employ civilian labour; they already had a supply in the cavalry troopers. We were the builders.

I don't recall anything of the march to Lancaster, but I do remember the aftermath. It was one of the most stubborn battles I ever took part in against the Indians, and one I was fortunate to survive.

I had hardly arrived at Lancaster when the warning came. I had corralled my horse, and the bugle thrilled through the camp and partly-built fort, calling us all to arms. There is nothing quite like the feeling that a battle is imminent. The blood flows faster, the heart-beat increases, and one feels entirely alive, yet simultaneously, one has a sinking, gut-wrenching feeling of fear, mingled with the terrible knowledge that you could be dead before the sun sets.

We ran to grab our Spencers and hastened to our allocated stations. I was fortunate that William was my right-hand man, for one needs to know one's companions in a fight. Having trust in one's comrades is half the battle. Without trust, one gets nervous, and a soldier looking over his shoulder is a soldier contemplating retreat or defeat. At that time Lancaster was a fort only in name, for we were still erecting the place, so we were camped in the open, without even a stockade to provide shelter. I saw the cloud of dust in the distance, advancing toward us at some speed.

"How many do you reckon?" the captain asked, pretending nonchalance but chewing his tobacco at great speed to give the lie to his act. His name was William Frohock, a good man and a soldier.

"Three, mebbe four hundred," Sergeant Greaves said.

"How 'bout you?" The captain nodded to me. "I hear you were in the War."

"I'd agree," I said. "About four hundred, coming fast."

"They ain't no trading party then," the captain said. "Form a hollow square, boys, and keep your powder dry."

There were 40 of us, and the patrol that came in with me was weary. We did not know who the enemy was or why they were attacking us. We only knew we had to fight for our lives.

"Let them see who we are," Captain Frohock said and thrust Company K's standard right in the middle of us. If I close my eyes, I can see it yet, standing proud amidst the black-faced troopers in blue. I was as proud of that standard as if I had given birth to it and vowed to fight for Company K.

"Them's Kickapoos," Frohock told us. "I didn't know they could muster that many braves."

They were stubborn, these Kickapoos, and fought us in a series of charges that lasted a full three hours. I heard later that there were more than 900 attacking us, a devil's mixture of Kickapoos, Mexicans, Lipans and white American outlaws. I can neither confirm the numbers nor who they were. I can only say I thought they were all Indians, and all I saw was a horde of yelling, hate-twisted faces. As always in battle, the time passed very quickly and left me with only a series of disjointed images.

I remember squeezing my trigger and having it click on an empty rifle. I remember loading with such haste that I nearly fumbled the cartridges, with one screaming Kickapoo only a few yards away. I remember a pause in the fighting, with powder smoke curling around us, and William calmly stuffing tobacco in his pipe. He pushed back his hat and winked at me.

"When we're in Africa," he said, "we'll tell this tale to our grandchildren."

I was panting then, fighting for breath, and thirsty. I always got thirsty in battle; maybe it was the powder smoke, or maybe my nerves. I took a drink from my canteen and returned William's smile.

"Here they come again," Lieutenant Frohock said. "Get ready, boys!"

We got ready. It was a cool day for such a hot fight, and overcast, so I heard later. I don't remember it as such. I remember the glint of sun on metal, the sweat running down my back and the scream one of our men made as he was shot. He fell, writhing, with his boots kicking up the dust as he kicked in his agony.

"Leave him," Frohock said. "We'll attend to him later. "We need every rifle facing forward."

The Kickapoos launched attack after attack, losing men to our Spencers, and with their battle whoops and screams shrill in our ears. Our young soldiers did themselves proud that day, and I shot at least two of the Kickapoos. When they retired, licking their wounds and carrying their wounded with them, we found the bodies of twenty of their number on the ground and were satisfied.

I thought we only lost a single man. I was wrong. It was not until the Kickapoos retreated that I realised we had lost three of our own. The Kickapoos had shot one man beside me, one man had been guarding the herds and had vanished, while the third had disappeared, nobody knew where.

That third man was William Sharpe, the best man I have ever known.

Sometimes, after a battle, you will hear men boasting of the deeds they have done and of the enemy they have killed. The veterans did not do that. If they are like me, they do not remember, for a battle is always chaotic and a trooper's view is limited to a few square yards, wreathed by smoke, clouded by dust and shrouded in excitement. Oh, there is fear too, but not as much as the recruit expects. There is fear before action, but when one is fighting, you are too busy for fear. Afterwards, when you lie alone at night under the stars, and the wind rustles the brush, you remember and lie in your own cold sweat.

Not William though. William always slept like a baby afterwards. I lay under the Texas skies, wondering where he was. He was officially posted as missing believed dead, and we harboured slender hopes that he would turn up somewhere. Unofficially, we all knew the Kickapoos had taken him. I remembered the solemn oath William and I had made not to let the Indians capture one another. I begged Lieutenant Frohock to take out a patrol to search for William.

"It's too dangerous, trooper," Frohock said. "There's less than 40 of us left now, with barely enough ammunition to beat off one determined attack, and hundreds of hostiles waiting somewhere in the brush. They'd love to see a small patrol ride into their hands."

I knew the lieutenant was right. I knew it was plain foolish to diminish our numbers further, but William had been my friend. I owed him my life and more. Later, much later, when reinforcements reached Fort Lancaster, we found all that remained of William Sharpe. The Kickapoos had blinded him, castrated and scalped him and shot a dozen arrows into his tortured body. I wept when I found him, openly and without shame as the other troopers watched, some with understanding, and others without. I did not care what they thought.

It was many years since I had last cried, and it was many years before I would cry again.

I FIGHT ALONG THE FRONTIER

*I*never felt quite the same after the death of William Sharpe. The Army lost its flavour for me, like beef without salt. I had lost colleagues before, of course, especially during the great Civil War, when we could share a mug of coffee at sundown and find them stiff, twisted and dead of disease in the dawning. We learned to treat death as only another companion on the long trail to freedom and greet him as an invisible presence in the ranks. William was different. We had been more than just colleagues; we had been friends, brothers-in-arms, brothers in everything except blood. I missed him then, and I miss him all these long years later.

When we found William, the Kickapoos had left his pipe behind. They had decorated William's body obscenely with his prized possession. I rescued that pipe with its elaborate African carvings and its long curved stem, and I have it still. It sits beside me as I write, a visible reminder of the best friend a man could ever have.

Strangely, after William's death, Sergeant Greaves stopped hazing me. Perhaps he knew I no longer cared about life and death and would have plunged a knife into his body without concern about the hangman's noose. I went wild for a spell. I replaced my friendship with William with love for whiskey, and I argued and fought with my fellow soldiers. They learned to avoid me as I became morose, a man alone who muttered into the neck of a bottle and glowered at the world through bitter, bloodshot eyes. I placed William's pipe beneath my pillow and muttered revenge, although who I wished vengeance on, I do not know.

However, I had little time to mourn as the next year saw the 9th ride and fight and chase all across Texas to the banks of the Rio Grande. Joining the Kickapoos, the Comanche and Mescaleros added fire to the heat that consumed the frontier country. I played my part as a trooper, never distinguishing myself, never running from danger, doing my duty and little else.

1869 was no better. I spent much of that year in the saddle, without any success. For me, it was a year to forget. The 9th had one signal success. Captain Henry Carroll and 95 men located a large gathering of Kiowas and Comanches at the headwaters of the Salt Fork River and charged them in the old traditional style. I heard that bugles were blaring and the guidon flying high as the 9th carved their way through the enemy. It was a fine victory, but I was not involved. I was on the banks of the Rio Grande at the time, staring across the muddy waters and wondering about deserting to Mexico.

I was still morose and withdrawn, doing no more than my duty, participating in the occasional skirmish and hoping to meet the Kickapoos who murdered William. Perhaps I did; I will never know. I must have caught somebody's eye for one of the officers reported me to the colonel as an experienced soldier with potential. God only knows what potential I had.

Colonel Hatch was as frustrated as the rest of us by the constant raiding of the Indian tribes, and he decided to end the menace. Hatch's first move was to promote me to corporal, which must have terrified the Indians. His next was to send Captain John Bacon, a Kentucky man, to Fort Concho with picked men from six companies. Despite my sullen demeanour and new promotion, Hatch selected me as one of the men. Perhaps he thought the dazzle from my pristine stripes would overawe the Apaches.

We were the pick of the 9th, the best Buffalo Soldiers in all of Texas. And every one of us, except me, knew it. We wanted to whip the Indians and whip them good. In early October 1869, we marched to the Brazos River and the wind-haunted site of Fort Phantom Hill, where a patrol of the 4th Cavalry waited for us. We also had a dozen or so Tonkawa Indians as scouts. The men of the 4th did not seem pleased to see the black faces of the 9th, but we did not care. We were the Buffalos, better soldiers than the 4th would ever be.

"Ignore the jibes," Captain Bacon said. "The men of the 4th are our allies and friends."

I reinforced that message to the men under my command. "Don't get into fights with the 4th," I said. "The man you punch might hold the rifle that kills the Indian who wants your scalp."

My men listened. They knew I was a veteran and also knew I would knock them down if they disobeyed me.

We were about 200 strong, I reckon, or maybe slightly less, when Captain Bacon marched us towards the headquarters of the hostiles. We had not broken camp on that October morning when the Indians attacked in their hundreds. I said then, and reckon still, that our Tonkwana scouts informed the hostiles of our intentions. A united force of Kiowa and Comanche came with the rising sun at their back, and our proposed offensive operation quickly became a desperate defence.

"Stay with me, William," I pleaded, fingering William's pipe.

There was a hard battle of rifle and arrow and at times tomahawk and pistol. Outnumbered at least two-to-one and fighting on ground with which the Indians were familiar, we fired and fought like the veterans we were.

I will not describe that battle. To me, most fights with the Indians were the same. Either we galloped towards them and had a running skirmish from horseback, or we were on foot in a rough square or circle, and they were charging towards us, shrieking and hollering. This encounter was the latter kind of battle, and our blue troopers fought off the Indians. One moment the enemy was a shrieking band of warriors, and the next they were running.

"Thank you, William," I said to his pipe. William did not reply.

Captain Bacon did not give the Indians time to reform. "Mount up!" he roared, with his Kentucky accent so strong I could taste the whiskey. "Mount up, form ranks and chase them redskins to Kingdom Come and beyond!"

"You heard the captain!" I said to my men. I think that was when the worst pain of William's death began to ease. It continued to hurt – it still does – but as a dull ache in my heart rather than an over-riding agony that felt like the Kickapoos were thrusting their torture knives into my guts.

Next day, we located the hostile's camp. Our tame Tonkwanas pointed out the hostiles, grinning as if they had done something special, rather than doing their duty, and Captain Bacon lined us up on the far side of a ridge and gave brief instructions.

"The hostiles are over that ridge," he said, looking at us one at a time. "When the bugle calls, we are going to cross the ridge and ride down upon them. I want no hesitation, boys, and no thoughts of false mercy. Think what they would do if the position were reversed and destroy them."

I nodded, touched William's pipe and repeated the order to my men. "Kill them all," I said.

We lined up, walked our horses to the top of the ridge and looked down upon our enemy.

"Bugler," Bacon said softly, "sound the charge."

A bugle call is like no other sound in the world. It can be heard a mile away and penetrates even the roar of battle to give orders to the troops where no human voice could carry. The sound of the charge is the most thrilling sound a cavalry trooper can ever hear. It still resounds in my head, as does the image of these 200 troopers, black and white together, advancing under the guidons. I held the memory of the horrors the Indians unleashed in my head.

"Charge!" I shouted, as the whole line of troopers moved forward, slowly at first and gathering momentum as we descended that dusty, stony ridge. The bugle continued, with the calls thrilling us to action and the Indians either staring at us in astonishment or scattering before us. At that stage, I did not care whether I lived or died. The bugle has that effect; it is the most martial sound one can imagine.

"William!" I shouted then. "For you, William!"

I spurred ahead of my men, guiding my horse with my knees as I held my Spencer in both hands. The image of William was in my head, William laughing, William drunken, William cavorting with a harlot and his backside in the air, and then William as I saw him last, tortured to a foul death. I showed no mercy to the Indians. I shot all I saw, men and women, killing them without compulsion. I know that people will find it wrong that I shot women, but it was the women who often inflicted the worst tortures on prisoners. I thought of William and saw that Indian encampment through a red haze of rage and blood.

"Corporal!" I felt a hand on my sleeve. "Corporal!"

I looked around with my head slowly clearing. Captain Bacon was beside me, one hand on my arm and concern in his eyes. "He's dead, corporal. You can stop now."

I nodded. "Yes, sir." I must have dismounted, although I did not know when. I was in the middle of a pile of dead Indian bodies, crashing the stock of my carbine onto the skull of a corpse.

Captain Bacon continued to watch me for the remainder of that day, then other things took his interest, and I was free to resume my ordinary duties as a corporal.

I remained under Bacon's command that winter, riding and

patrolling against the Mescalero Apaches and Comanches south-west of Fort McKavett. We had female laundresses at this fort, and I became quite attached to one, a mixed-race Mexican with a big smile and wide hips. We were sufficiently friendly that I thought of marriage, for she was a good cook as well as a willing bed partner, but she dismissed my tentative approaches with a laugh.

"Little black babies," she said. "I don't want little black babies."

After that rebuff, I turned my attention elsewhere.

I cannot recall any specific event of that season except a picture in my mind of one day when two Buffalo Soldiers stood on the skyline. Each man held his horse, and the sun was setting in that glorious way that only Texas can give. One Buffalo Soldier was facing away from me, watching the ground for any Apache or Comanche, and the other was in profile. He was a typical 9th Cavalryman, medium height, with his hat pulled low over his head and his uniform faded by the weather, a stubby clay pipe in his mouth, water bottle at his hip and the Spencer in his right hand.

That image epitomized the 9th for me. Black men in blue uniforms working and fighting together in a vast landscape, for little pay and less gratitude. I can see those men now and retain a feeling of pride at having been a Buffalo Soldier.

I had one other memorable Indian encounter when I was under Captain Bacon's command. It was in May 1870, a week or so before the 9th transferred me elsewhere. I was attached to Company F at that time, still a corporal, and Sergeant Stance led a ten-man patrol out of Fort McKavett on a routine scouting mission. We were not searching for anything in particular but were always wary of trouble. We had to be ready in Old Texas.

We rode north along the Kickapoo Road, with the sky a blue abyss above us and the horses warm and willing underneath. I had volunteered for this mission, mainly because the Kickapoos had been active recently, and I had never forgiven them for the torture of William. Death in battle was part of the contract, but foul death under torture was something different. The Kickapoos around Fort McKavett had kidnapped children from various ranches, and if our patrol came across any news of the kidnappings, we were to investigate. In my mind, that meant pursue the raiders and kill them all.

Rather than locate missing children, when we were about fifteen miles north of McKavett, we ran into a Kickapoo band with a herd of horses. Stance thought the horses might be entirely legitimate until the Kickapoos edged away from us.

"Where did you get those horses?" Sergeant Stance asked, and the Indians presented their rifles. I had expected nothing else from Kickapoos and fired first; the Indians retaliated, and we charged. Before we reached them, the Kickapoos wheeled their ponies around and high-tailed it, leaving us with nine stolen horses as prizes.

We camped for the night at nearby Kickapoo Springs, with the captured horses beside our own. We kept men on guard in case the Kickapoos tried to recapture the horses, but it was uneventful. Stance had us up and saddled before six the next day, and we headed for Fort McKavett, reasonably pleased with ourselves, although we had not found the missing children. Sergeant Stance was an experienced man and sent scouts out ahead, with one galloping back to tell us there was another party of Kickapoos a mile or so down the road.

We rode up without making a noise and watched the Indians for a spell. After a few minutes, we saw rising dust as two wagons rolled towards the fort.

Stance looked us over. "Well, boys," he said. "We see the enemy, and we see what they're planning. Bugler, sound the charge!"

The Kickapoos did not expect us, but to give them justice, they kept their discipline and tried to escape, taking another herd of stolen horses with them.

"Open fire, boys!" Stance ordered, and we did so. When the

bullets started buzzing, the Kickapoos abandoned the horses and fled. Stance added the newly-captured horses to ours, and we rode on. The Kickapoos soon recovered and, seeing how few we were, they followed us, keeping to the brush along our left flank. Stance kept us together until we reached a water hole when we turned at bay. We remained together, scattering the Indians with volley fire until they retreated into the backcountry. We brought our captured horses into the fort without further incident. For his leadership, Stance earned the Medal of Honor. I heard that another patrol found the kidnapped children, but I was not part of that expedition.

Late in December 1870, Lieutenant-Colonel Merritt replaced Hatch in command of the 9th. I watched Colonel Hatch ride out with mixed feelings, for he was a good soldier and a good officer. I stood at the gate and saluted and, gentleman that he was, Colonel Hatch halted his horse, faced me squarely and returned my salute, man-to-man. I will never forget that gesture of respect.

I continued to be a good soldier while on active service but became troublesome when in barracks. I lost my stripes when I brawled with a trooper and regained them after a stiff march in the White Sands region. I had no sooner got used to my chevrons when I was once more busted to a private trooper and awarded six weeks hard labour for telling Sergeant Greaves to get to Hell and stay there. It looked like I was destined to remain at the lowest rank during my time in the 9th.

With Mexicans raiding from over the Rio Grande, and Apaches killing and stealing at will, 1872 was a violent year along the frontier. That year I was based at Fort Clark, now a hard-bitten, hard-drinking member of a veteran regiment. I was out with the patrol that found the remains of a contractor's train on the San Antonio to El Paso road. I was in Company A then, under the command of Captain Michael Cooney. He was a red-haired Irishman who retained the Paddy in his voice and fire in his belly despite many years of experience.

We had all seen the results of Indian raids, with scalped men and women, but that train sticks in my memory.

"Let's catch these bastards, boys," Cooney said. If you had ever heard an Irish veteran say those words, you would know the meaning of the word menace.

We agreed, wordless as we examined the handiwork of the Indian band. The smell of burning human flesh hung heavy in the air, alongside the charred, twisted horrors that only 24 hours before had been living, laughing men and women.

The Indians had swooped on the train before the travellers could defend themselves, and had captured most of the civilians involved. Any traveller, pilgrim or trader in west Texas should hire a decent quota of guards, for these arid plains hold some of the most predatory killers on earth. I have heard that people now look on the American Indians as heroes, brave men defending their lands, and the tribes may genuinely have been defending their way of life. We of the Buffalo Soldiers did not view them like that.

To us, the Indians were a savage and unrelentingly cruel enemy that exploded from their reservations and fastnesses onto the nearly defenceless civilian population of Texas to murder, rape, loot and torture. They liked to attack small army patrols, but very rarely fought unless they were in overwhelming strength.

In this case, the Indians had killed women and children as well as men. The civilians had not died quickly, and they had not died well. The Indians had tied men to the wheels of the wagons and slowly burned them to death, so it was with iron in our hearts that we followed the raiders.

As we rode, I fingered Will's pipe and promised revenge on these murdering savages.

Company H joined us soon after, and we combined our forces to track and pursue the murderers. At that time, many of our veterans had left the 9th, and young, untried recruits filled the uniforms. I was one of the oldest and most experienced men there and tried to teach the greenhorns how to be soldiers even as we rode. We were in columns of two as we rode into a rocky valley, a long blue snake with the guidon flying before us and vengeance in our hearts.

The Indians were waiting. They had dug trenches on the rocky sides of the valley and had hidden themselves so well that our earliest warning was the sound of their rifles. Captain Cooney was one of the first to fall, with his horse dead beneath him, or on top of him, rather, for it pinned him as it collapsed. Another eight horses died or lay screaming and kicking in the dust as the acrid gun smoke drifted across the valley. Before the recruits recovered from their initial shock, we saw Cooney's injured horse struggling to its feet. It ran in pain-created panic, dragging the captain behind it. If you think you know what swearing is, try listening to an excited Irish soldier as a wounded horse pulls him across rough ground. I had no idea a man could fit so many obscenities into such a short space of time.

I ran to help, but Private Isaac Harrison got there first, grabbing at the horse's reins while Trumpeter William Nelson cut Cooney free.

Shaken and bruised but still very much in command, Cooney ordered us back from the ambush. We withdrew sullenly, hating to be bested by a bunch of savages.

"Dismount," Cooney ordered, with a trickle of blood running down his face. He pulled his revolver from its holster, checked the chambers to ensure it was loaded, and gestured back to the ambush. He gave us a sudden grin. "We're going back in, lads. Follow me."

Like all the best captains, Cooney led from the front. We followed, finding cover among the hot, dry rocks, ducking whenever we heard the crack of an Indian's rifle, creeping forward slowly. We were intent on revenging our earlier reverse. All the while, the Indians' bullets whined and screamed among us, pinging from the rocks, ricocheting dangerously and raising chips and spurts of dust. Not all the bullets missed. The Indians shot Lieutenant Vincent of H Company, wounding him in both legs. I heard Vincent cry out at the impact of the shot, and saw his blood steaming in the heat, but he refused to retire. He kept moving with his face to the enemy.

Whatever people can say against the officers of the 9th Cavalry, there was no doubting their courage. I never saw any hint of cowardice among them at any time in my service.

Raw soldiers cannot capture a strong position defended by stubborn, skilled men without overwhelming numbers or a flanking attack. Captain Cooney sounded the retreat, giving the victory to the Indians. With no water and little ammunition remaining, we left that valley. Dark had fallen by then, and Lieutenant Vincent was dying through shock and loss of blood as we retreated with our heads down and shoulders bowed. That was the only defeat I remember with the 9th, although we did not always succeed in catching the marauding bands.

There were other skirmishes, such as the occasion when a detachment of Company D rode into Fort Stockton with every man wearing an Indian bonnet they had captured from a camp. Nobody was injured in that bloodless victory, and the sight raised our morale.

Although the civil war had now been over for some seven years, men in blue uniforms were still not popular in Texas, despite the efforts of the 9th and other regiments to defend them. We had saved Texans from Apaches, Mexicans, Kiowas, Comanches and various outlaw bands, with little gratitude. Black men in blue uniforms were particularly unwelcome.

When we caught outlaws, the civilian courts often set them free, much to our frustration. Some of the troopers wondered if it was worthwhile bringing men to such justice. Some of us wanted to hang them, there and then, or shoot them out of hand. I was one of these men, for I had witnessed too many brave men die to wish to set gun runners, murderers and their friends free. However, we did not dispense instant justice. We were professional soldiers, earning our $13 a month the only way we knew how.

In 1874, I was based at Camp Ringgold, square on the Mexican border, for a spell. This camp is on the north bank of the Rio Grande, in Starr County, which was a rough, tough border area, fiercely independent of anybody, particularly the federal government. The men here did not fear the Union, the Mexicans, God, the devil or even the 9th Cavalry. It was in Camp Ringgold that some of the younger, greener, soldiers fell victim to the hordes of professional gamblers. These predators waited until payday then lured in the boys with promises of riches, whiskey and women. They allowed the youngsters to win a few hands of cards, convinced them they were good players, then gradually robbed them of everything the troopers had, leaving some boys so deeply in debt they would have to serve years to break even.

By this time, Colonel Hatch had returned to command and arrested one of the most prominent of the gamblers. The gambler appeared before Starr County court, who backed him. Many people in the one-star State of Texas still resented the blue-coated defenders of its people and security, whatever the colour of their skin. Possibly adherence to the Confederacy influenced this animosity, although I don't believe so. I think that the Starr County people had a deeper, older loyalty to their Mexican roots. The county is right on the Mexican border, and the majority of the population are of Mexican origin.

That anti-blue situation became evident when a cavalry patrol out of Ringgold came under attack at a Sonis Ranch, Starr County. Usually, we expected Comanches or Apaches to be the enemy, but in Starr the ranchers themselves attacked us. Two of our young soldiers, Moses Turner, a serious, intelligent boy, and Jerry Owsley, whom I did not know, died and two others fled into the surrounding brush. More experienced men might have fared better, but that is speculation from a veteran. Sergeant Troutman, in charge of the patrol, returned to Ringgold with news of the ambush but without his men.

I was not involved in the ambush, so don't know the details. Nor was I part of the patrol next day, which, if my memory is accurate, Colonel Hatch led in person. The patrol found Turner and Owsley, naked and butchered. Memories of William's death flooded back to me as 9th Cavalry seethed with anger. To be murdered by the very people we were trying to protect was the ugliest of deaths.

Colonel Hatch's patrol arrested a bunch of Mexicans for the murders and dragged them back to Ringgold. When the colonel handed the suspects to the civil authorities in Rio Grande City, the civilians released eight of them without charge. The ninth faced a mockery of a trial, then was acquitted.

The death of two troopers of the 9th meant nothing to the authorities of Starr County. The anger of the 9th increased when the civic authorities arrested the soldiers who spoke at the trial and accused them of murdering one of the attackers. The civilians also threatened to prosecute the colonel for illegally searching the barns. Hatch spent a lot of money in hiring a good attorney who successfully defended him, but the resentment remained within us. Even today, mention of Starr County brings bitter memories to my mind.

I LEAVE THE BUFFALO SOLDIERS

My time with the Buffalo Soldiers was coming to an end, and Starr County hastened my departure. There had been rumours that the government planned to move the 9th away from Texas to New Mexico, but we tried to ignore them. We had been on the frontier for so long we felt like a permanent presence. Many men joined the regiment, served all their time on the Rio Grande and left without knowing anywhere else. I was a corporal and did not expect to reach any higher rank, a grizzled veteran of about 28, bitter-eyed and cynical about everything under the harsh Texan sun.

I was leading a small patrol of ten men around the outlying ranches, investigating reports of Mexican raiders, fully aware that their cousins and friends in Starr would never give them up. We rounded up a herd of stolen horses and were returning to Ringgold when one of my men, Trumpeter Whyte, saw a suspicious cloud of dust rising to the east.

Dust can tell an experienced man a great deal. A large cloud, slow-moving, could indicate a herd of cattle, while fast-rising dust suggests a group of raiders if it's across country, or a cavalry patrol if it follows the line of a road. This cloud was fast and did not follow the line of any road.

"Shall we investigate?" Whyte asked, and I decided we should. Rather than split my small command in the face of a possible hostile force, I kept us all together. Mexicans or Indians love to attack lone troopers or pairs of troopers.

As we suspected, a party of raiders created the dust. They were mixed whites and Mexicans, driving horses they had stolen from the Kiowa. That is an aspect of Texas that people did not often mention; the Indian tribes could be victims as well as aggressors, and it was the 9th's duty to protect them as much as anybody else. When we intercepted the rustlers, they proved to outnumber us by three to one, and after the recent encounter at Sonis Ranch, they were happy to fight back. Nevertheless, I thought it best to show a bold face and bluff our way out of trouble.

I certainly had no intention of retreating from such a bunch of Border scum, and formed my men in a line, facing the raiders. As the dust settled around us, I demanded that the rustlers hand over the stolen horses so the 9th could return them to the proper owners.

The leader of the raiders looked at me and counted my men. He could see that his men outnumbered mine. He could also see that my men held their rifles in their hands, ready to fire. If he were looking properly, he would see me glance to the scrub-covered ridge at my back. If he were a sensible man, he would wonder why I glanced there and would wonder how many men I had hidden, ready to pounce on his thieving band.

The situation was tense, with the rustlers sitting on a hair-trigger and my men eager for blood after the recent murder of their colleagues. I could see the raiders reaching for pistol and rifle, and prepared to give the order to open fire. Only the arrival of a war party of Kiowas saved the day from descending into mass slaughter.

The yip-yip-yip of the Indians and the sight of their weapons turned the tide in our favour. The raiders turned their horses around, kicked in their spurs and fled, not all in the same direction. We handed the horses to the Kiowa, who seemed surprised, and we returned to the fort. We were quite satisfied with the outcome. We had not only recovered stolen horses and stopped a likely retaliatory raid by the Kiowa, but we had also returned without a casualty.

I was not so contented two days later when the civil authorities in Rio Grande City placed me under arrest. They charged me with horse-stealing and escorted me to the local lock-up, with great ceremony and much mockery. In the morning, I was a proud corporal of the 9th Cavalry, and in the afternoon, I was a prisoner in the Rio Grande jail, lying with manacles on my wrists. I will swear to this day that one of my jailers was part of the raider gang that stole the Kiowa's horses. The only solace I had was William's pipe, which was inside my tunic. As long as I had that with me, I knew I was not alone. William was looking after me, despite my leaving him for the Kickapoos to torture.

I fretted in jail, particularly when one man, my raider friend, told me that the penalty for horse-stealing was death. He made a neat little hangman's noose, which he suspended from his belt whenever he came into my cell.

"We're going to hang you," he told me.

I said nothing, for I suspected that he was correct. Starr County did not like the 9th Cavalry and I did not expect to find justice in their court. I was wrong. Colonel Hatch hired a very able legal counsel to argue my case. I can say that standing in the dock terrified me more than facing the Confederates at the Crater, for I was unarmed and unjustly accused, while dependant for my life and liberty on a man I did not know. I should have had more faith in the colonel.

My counsel argued and won. When I heard the verdict of not guilty, I nearly collapsed where I stood. I hoped that was the end of the matter, but the Starr County men disagreed with the verdict. I had no sooner left the court than what appeared to be half the population of Rio Grande City surged around me.

"Hang him!" somebody shouted, and others joined in.

"Hang him!"

There were women as well as men amongst the mob that laid hands on me. I knocked down the first and the second, and I think the third, but after that their numbers overwhelmed me.

"Hang him!" a man roared and grabbed me around the neck.

"Hang him!" a spotty-faced youth screamed, high pitched.

Above the heads of the crowd, I saw a man toss a rope over the branch of a tree. As the mob pushed me onward, the rope-man formed a neat noose, which was a sight I never want to see again.

A soldier's life on the Texas frontier could end at any time. That is part of the contract. That is why the trooper pockets his $13 a month. Even so, I did not want to die at the hands of a maniacal mob. Calming my panic with an effort, I called on my years of military experience to help me. I looked around, searching for an escape from this ambush, and I saw my chance. One of my captors had carelessly allowed his revolver holster to come close to me. I think my guardian angel was hovering above my head, pointing his celestial finger, or perhaps it was William Sharpe. I remember every detail of that weapon. It was an 1848 Pocket Colt, old fashioned, with silvered brass grip straps, circular cylinder stops and squareback trigger guard. The handle was of plain walnut, worn by use and it was only six inches from my right hand. It was the act of an instant to relieve the man of his burden and fire it.

As three men held me, I could not lift my arm, which meant I fired into the ground. The bullet thudded into the dirt, hit a stone with an amazingly bright spark, and ricocheted horizontally. It passed through the calf of a plump Mexican and landed in the left buttock of the spotty youth who had gleefully wanted to hang me. That single shot brought instant pandemonium. Women screamed, men yelled and ran, or turned toward me in consternation.

"He's got a gun!" somebody pointed out, and the remaining

mob instantly broke, to scatter in every direction. Only the two wounded men lay on the ground, with the Mexican trying to crawl away and the youth babbling and howling with both hands on his torn buttock. I ran, still holding the Baby Colt. Only one man returned to try and restrain me. He snarled drunkenly and tried to swing the Springfield rifle from his shoulder. It was either instinct or training that made me fire first. When I saw the scarlet blood spurt from the man's chest, I knew at once that my adversary was dead and people would call me a murderer.

In that short space of time, the crowd had reassembled at the fringes of the street. The men gave a great roar of rage, and one or two began to fire at me, although I have no idea where their bullets went. I did not care, as long as they missed me. I ran for my life, with no thought except for the immediate present. I forgot the regiment and everything else as I shoved through the streets with the remnants of the mob either fleeing or trying to stop me.

A score of hands clutched at me, mostly men but also some woman. An elderly Mexican woman swung a broom at my head, another thrust a long pole at my groin; both missed, fortunately. I punched somebody – man or woman, I did not know – stabbed straight fingers into a lean man's throat, felt nails rake down my face and broke free of the despairing clutch of a swearing man. With no thought except escape, I ran into the brush, pursued by a dozen or so men and women, all hollering in excitement.

"Shoot him!" somebody yelled in Spanish, and half a dozen shots sounded.

`"You got him!" a woman screeched, also in Spanish. "I saw the blood spurt."

Unwounded, I kept moving. I was a hardened, fit, experienced soldier with a five-shot revolver in my fist, a killer and veteran. I was also a lone black man in a blue uniform in an area where neither black men nor blue uniforms were welcome. I ran for a mile, weaving and ducking in case somebody had drawn a bead on me. The would-be lynch-mob was yelling behind me, their voices growing fainter by the minute until I heard the drumbeat of hooves and knew that horsemen had joined my pursuers. That was bad medicine. I could outrun any number of civilians, but I knew that riders would run me down in minutes.

I halted, with the breath rasping in my throat and my hands shaking from reaction. I decided that it would be better to die fighting than to have a mob of Border cut-throats rope me and drag me to a hanging tree. I stood with my back to a white pine tree, still in uniform except for my hat, facing my pursuers. When they saw me waiting, they dismounted and spread out, grinning, encouraging each other with loud shouts, mainly in Spanish but with some American as well.

"He's stopped at a tree!"

"A hanging tree!"

"Get him, boys! He's only got one gun, and he's fired twice already."

I checked the chambers of my Colt. I had three bullets, three for a dozen men and two women, so even if I dropped three with three shots, I would still have nine men and two women to face. That was bad odds.

"Who's got the rope?" a big-bellied, bearded man asked. He waddled closer, pulling a long-barrelled Colt from its holster.

"I've got it!" a skinny runt of a man said. They all spoke in Spanish now. Mexicans too, a man and woman, they circled me warily. Sure enough, the runt carried a length of thin rope coiled over his shoulder. The mob edged closer, encouraging each other with loud voices, and the women urging them forward, pushing their men into danger. They were the trash of Texas, the refuse of the Border, bully-boys and ten-to-one murderers. I waited, saying nothing, thinking my life would end soon, watching my enemies and very aware that there was nobody to help me. The 9th Cavalry would not ride over the hill to my rescue.

In any crowd or gang, there will be a man the others look to, a natural leader. He will have one or two close associates upon whom he depends, and the bulk of the others will be trash. They will be nothing without the leader. The only plan I had was to kill the leaders, and to do that, I had to identify them.

"Who's first?" I challenged them in Spanish, for after serving years along the Rio Grande frontier, I was fluent in that language. Anyway, I was a quick learner where languages were at stake. I brandished my Colt. "I've got six men's lives in here."

That was a blatant lie, for my revolver was a five-shooter, and I had already emptied two chambers. I had no spare cartridges with me, and the 1848 Pocket Colt was notoriously difficult to load. The model did not come with a loading lever, so to reload, I would have to remove the barrel wedge, then take off the barrel and the cylinder. After that, I'd have to charge each cylinder with gunpowder, add a bullet and ram them in place. Only then could I place a percussion cap over each cone and reassemble the gun with the barrel wedge. Yet still the procedure was not complete, for I'd have to rotate the cylinder until the revolver's hammer sat over a safety pin at the rear facing. It was a lengthy procedure that I had neither time nor the inclination to perform. In my opinion, the Pocket Colt belonged in a museum.

My attackers opened fire, with the bullets whistling past my head or thudding into the tree at my back. I crouched and ducked behind the tree, wishing the Kiowa Indians would appear to rescue me, or William would return from the dead.

"He's yellow!" the big-bellied man roared.

"No," an unshaven white American said in fluent Spanish, "he's jest taking cover. Go slow. Spread out further, boys, and we'll outflank him. Block his retreat."

There he was; there was the leader. The unshaven American was my first target. I circled the tree, moving erratically to disrupt my attackers' aims, always watching the unshaven American. The two women were screaming abuse, ordering the men to kill me and threatening me with obscene methods of death.

The mob was now fifty yards away, with the unshaven white man moving purposefully towards me.

I should have been scared. I was not. My mind was working all the time, trying to find a stratagem to stop the mob from shooting me, while hoping for a clean shot at the leader.

Forty yards away, and they were swaggering, sure of their kill as they saw I was not going to run.

"If you throw down your gun, we'll kill you quick," the big-bellied man said. "If you don't, we hang you real slow above a fire." He went into details of what the women would do to me. The women laughed, adding horrors of their own.

They were thirty yards away, bunching for security and laughing harshly. I could see their faces, their eyes bright with anticipation. Two fired, with one shot hissing past and the other burrowing into the dirt at my feet. Thirty yards was a long range for a revolver, but if I waited for the mob to get closer, their shooting might improve, or they would rush me. After the big-bellied man's threats, I did not wish to entertain them by dancing at the wrong end of a rope, or worse.

Twenty-five yards and they began to increase their pace. I could not wait any longer. If I allowed them another ten paces, they would all come at once. Taking one step forward, I took deliberate aim at the unshaven man and pressed the trigger.

Every weapon has its peculiarities, and I did not know my stolen revolver. To increase my chances of a hit, I aimed at the buckle, right at the centre of the unshaven man's body. I heard the metallic clink as the lead bullet hit the brass buckle. The unshaven man staggered when my bullet hit home. He gave me a startled look and crumpled to the ground. I had hoped that his death would discourage the others. Instead, they surged forward, screaming in fury. I shot another, which left me with one bullet and ten men.

"I have four more bullets left," I shouted.

The mob was fifteen yards away. I forced myself to laugh, as though I did not care about death, and aimed at the man I considered the most significant threat. He hesitated when he saw me aim at him. I saw him falter, and I pressed the trigger. Once again, I aimed at the broadest part of his body and hit him in the stomach. His squeal rose above the roar of the others, and he fell, kicking and biting at the dust. The men on either side stopped, with one stooping to help, and the other stepping back.

Standing with an empty pistol, I could only bluff, as I had done so often around the poker table in frontier forts around Texas. There was one difference; in the 9th, I would have lost a few dollars, while here, my life was at stake.

"Kill him!" one of the women screamed.

Holding my empty revolver, I aimed at the next man, the bearded, big-bellied loudmouth, and I smiled full in his eyes.

He hesitated, looked over his shoulder at his writhing, screaming companion, turned and fled. His example spread to the men on either side of him. They faltered, and when I aimed at the thin man with the rope, he also ran. The rest followed, except for the women, who pointed and screamed at me before joining the others. Some mounted their horses, others forgot them in their panic.

I had bluffed my way to victory but did not stay long to savour the feeling. Dropping my now empty Pocket Colt, I lifted an Army Colt from the fat bearded man and took his cartridge belt into the bargain. The other casualties furnished me with a water bottle and more ammunition.

"Gracias," I said and whistled up two of the stray horses. After years as a cavalryman, I knew all there was to know about horses. I took a few moments to adjust the saddle and speak to the horses before I mounted one and led the other. I had to move quickly, for as soon as the Texans, or Mexicans, gathered their courage, they would whistle up a posse and hunt me down.

I would be a hunted man now, as long as I was in Texas, or possibly as long as I was in the United States. As a lone man, I was only a speck in the vastness of Texas. In a land ravaged by Apaches, Kiowas, Comanches, Mexicans and outlaw bands, a single man is very vulnerable, and a lone black man doubly, trebly so. Every man's hand would be against me.

It was many years since I had been alone, and then only for a short time at the end of the Civil War. I wondered which way to ride. I could cross the Rio Grande into Mexico, where a black man was a rarity and bandits controlled much of the territory. I could head east or north, where black men were not so rare, but a larger population meant more law officers looking for me. I could head west, to Arizona and New Mexico and, eventually, California and a ship away from the United States.

Heading west would be a long, hard journey, yet I thought it best.

I WANDER ACROSS AMERICA

*T*he next few months were like nothing I experienced before, or since. I think I returned to a style of living that my ancestors – all our ancestors – experienced well back at the beginning of time. I thought of Adam and Eve in the Garden of Eden and how fortunate they were that God provided paradise for them, and how foolish they had been to throw it away due to the serpent's blandishments.

After years living on the Frontier, I was somewhat experienced in travelling in the wild places, and could look after myself outside civilisation, yet living within the supportive framework of the 9th Cavalry and living alone was vastly different. There were no ranting sergeants to ask for advice, no officers to take ultimate responsibility. I had to fend for myself, make my own choices and live with them if they were wrong. I also had to avoid people, both the settled and the wild, for I was a murderer and a deserter. As a black man on this wild frontier, every man's hand would be against me.

I headed north and then west, avoiding settlements, watching for stray bands of Apaches, Comanches and Kiowa and keeping well clear of the cavalry patrol routes. I slept away from my evening fire, in case it attracted prowlers, harboured my ammunition and lived as much with nature as I could. I learned to nurse my water and eat anything I could. Snakes and lizards were my prey, and any small animal I could find as I headed west, day after lonely day. When my boots wore out, I resoled them with the hide of a cow I killed on the fringe of some nameless ranch. I ate as much of the meat as I could, sun-dried what I could carry and rode on.

The days passed, each one taking me further from the land I knew, each mile taking me closer to California, my eventual goal.

At night, I held the long-stemmed pipe and spoke to William, who shared my camp.

"We'll laugh at this when we're home in Africa," I said, and he sat opposite me, a shadowy figure in the gloom.

William rode beside me by day, comforting me with his presence, and showed me where the sweet water rose. Together we watched the sun rise gloriously over the desert and heard the wind whisper across the vast southern prairies. We climbed the sierras where no black man had been before and saw wonders that would astonish God the creator.

I am not sure if I was insane in those days, or saner than I have ever been. It felt right to wander alone. I grew used to my own company, used to remaining in one place when the weather turned against me and eating things that would turn the stomach of any civilised man. I robbed an Apache camp for clothing once, washed out the crawling vermin at a water-hole and avoided the chase with ease.

Only twice in all these months did I speak to anybody. Once I accosted an itinerant blacksmith to renew the shoes on the horse, and once I found an Apache woman, thrown out by her tribe. The blacksmith looked terrified when I appeared in front of him, riding out of the desert like a black ghost. I had no money, so paid him with a warning of a war party of Kiowas and left as silently as I had arrived.

The woman was plump and unhappy, a squaw who had transgressed in some way. Her family had thrown her out to die in the wilderness. I took her with me for a few weeks, and we shared a bed at night and food during the day. We were never friendly, only using each other for comfort and survival. One night I decided I could not trust her anymore and left. Apache squaws can kill a man in a hundred painful ways. I do not know what happened to her.

I continued my journey, westward across America, avoiding the trails and travelling to places even the Indians did not know. I crossed mountain ranges and broad rivers, and eventually, months after I left the 9th, I came to signs of civilisation. I saw white men's farms and fences and stopped a ragged, bearded man, a wanderer like myself.

"Where am I?" I asked.

"California," he told me and walked off, heading north-east.

I continued into California until one night I saw the reflection of lights on the underside of the clouds above. "San Francisco," I told myself.

Before I left the wilds, I found a sheltered water-hole and stripped naked. I stood there, enjoying the sensation of the wind and sun caressing my body, then stepped in the water and washed the dust and dirt of my travels. I took my time, for I must have smelled like an old horse, and had no notion to repel the good citizens of Frisco with my aroma. I scrubbed every inch of myself with fine sand, from the top of my head to the soles of my feet, until my skin was raw and glowing. Once I finished washing, I cleaned my teeth with a twig, then used fingers of sand to burnish them.

Finally, and with great reluctance, I burned my travelling clothes. I piled them up in a pyramid and applied a flame, so they smouldered for a space and then burst into bright flames. I watched them burn with mixed emotions, for these clothes had served me well. When the fire died, and only ashes remained, I dressed again, donning what I hoped were respectable clothes I had bought from a trader some hundreds of miles back along the trail.

Then, respectable by my lights, I lifted William's pipe. "We're still together, old friend," I said. "I haven't forgotten about Africa."

William said nothing. I had not felt his presence for months and hoped he had not deserted me somewhere on the long trail across America.

I sold my faithful horses at a stable on the outskirts of San Francisco, sold the saddle and saddlebags at a loss and pocketed the money. I would not need a horse and saddle where I was headed. With my Springfield rifle over my shoulder, my Colt and knife on my belt and William's pipe safe inside my coat, I entered the city.

I MEET A FRIEND

I was not used to cities, and after so long out in the wilds, I was overawed. San Francisco was huge, terrifying to my eyes that were used to the wide-open spaces. I am sure I must have looked like the gullible little black boy I was, or the mountain man I had been. I stared at the crowds and the diverse people and contemplated turning back and returning to the wilderness. I felt as if I had entered the white man's world, and I knew I did not belong.

"Are you all right, boy?" The stocky man was so tanned it was hard to tell that he was white. He walked with an assured swagger, while his top hat sat at a jaunty angle on top of his head.

"I'm all right," I told him, keeping my head down for I was not used to human company.

"Where are you heading?" The stocky man fell into step beside me, walking with a peculiar rolling gait as if he were likely to fall with every step.

"I don't know," I said, wishing he would leave me in peace. "I was looking for a bed for the night and maybe the harbour."

"Ah," the stocky man said. "Do you know where to go?"

"No," I said shortly.

"I didn't think so," my new companion said. We were silent for a while, as we walked side by side, like old companions rather than strangers. The road was busy with wagons of every description, from long vehicles carrying new pilgrim settlers to wagons carrying lumber or kegs of spirits. Men on horseback rode past, some undoubtedly Mexican, others lean Americans. An occasional herd of cattle plodded along the street.

"You've come from the interior," the stocky man said.

"I have," I said, with my thumb hooked into my belt, ready to draw my revolver if this man proved hostile.

"Have you any money?" my companion asked.

"Some," I said, curling my fingers around the butt of my Colt.

"Not much, I reckon," my companion nodded to my Colt. "It's all right; I'm not interested in your money. I am interested in why a black man with trail dust on his boots and a cavalry swagger should be looking for a ship in 'Frisco, on the opposite coast from the Buffalo Soldiers' base."

I said nothing to that. I was not foolish enough to discuss my finances or history with a stranger, but his observation of my cavalry background shook me.

"You don't know where you are staying the night, do you?"

I admitted that I did not.

"That's what I thought. I know a place, a tight berth with a cheerful welcome, a glass of grog and," the stocky man gave me a sidelong look, "and a willing woman. What do you say?"

I had hardly seen a woman since my squaw, months ago, let alone a willing woman. With nothing better to do and no plans for the future except to survive the next day and a vague dream of reaching Africa, I agreed. After months living in the wilds, the offer of a bed and a woman was more temptation than I could withstand, and whatever this man offered would be better than a night lying on the sidewalk of a city.

Or so I reasoned.

"Peter Hayes!" My new friend held out his hand, with a smile on his face. "Pleased to meet you. Call me Peter."

"William Sharpe," I gave the name I had adopted. It was so long since I used my other name, I had almost forgotten what it was. Although I did not know if the authorities in Texas had contacted other states about me, I was not going to take a chance.

We shook hands, the black frontiersman and ex-Buffalo Soldier and the white man from San Francisco, and walked on together through the bustling city streets.

"We're going to meet a friend of mine," Peter Hayes said. "You'll like him. Everybody likes him."

I BECOME A SAILOR

*A*fter taking me through a confusion of streets, Peter brought me to a place called the Boston House, at the corner of Davis and Chambers streets. I was so near the waterfront that I could smell the sea and hear the scream of the seagulls. The sound of music and laughter greeted me as I stood in the street outside, with the bright lights of the bar inveigling me.

"Here we are," Peter said. "Our home from home for tired frontiersmen and weary sailors."

"I'd like to see the sea," I said. "I've never seen the sea."

Peter grinned. "Never? Come this way, William." Taking my arm in a friendly grip, he guided me to the waterfront. I looked upon a mass of ships and boats, with masts and spars and sails like a forest, a thing I had never seen before.

"I saw the Chesapeake once," I confessed, "during the War."

"You were a soldier?" Peter's eyes were shrewd.

"I was at the Crater," I said, remembering. "Does the Chesapeake count as the sea?"

"It sure does," Peter said, watching me.

"Then I've seen both of America's seas," I said. It was true. At the siege of Petersburg, I had glimpsed the Chesapeake, although I had never been to the coast. Now I had travelled the breadth of the United States from coast to coast. I wondered, silently, if any other black man had ever done such a thing.

"I'll take you again tomorrow," Peter said. "I promise."

That was one promise Peter kept.

"Come on now; the girls are waiting!" Wrapping an arm around my shoulder, he drew me back from the waterfront towards the Boston House. "Here we are."

Peter threw the door wide open and ushered me inside.

The noise was like an old friend, with the sweet smell of whiskey and the sweeter company of women. Lord, how I had missed the sound of a woman's laughter, the sight of a woman's smile and the sensation of a woman's body pressed close to mine. For a moment, I hesitated, for living alone for months had robbed me of many of the social graces, and then a waft of perfume came to me, a woman smiled in my direction, and I stepped inside.

The Boston House was like nowhere I had ever been. Men of all nationalities and none at all mixed together, black, white and Mexican. They sang songs I had never heard before, with words I did not understand, let alone know. These were seamen, speaking a language of their own: careless, happy-go-lucky men with battered faces and tattoos, rings in their ears and stories of places I did not know existed.

I sat in a corner with Peter at my side, listening to the conversation. These men spoke about ports in China and India, Australia and along the coast of South America, strange, exotic places with unfamiliar names. Scattered among the men were a dozen women, all gaudily dressed and friendly, like their kind always were.

Oh, I knew they were harlots, the kind of women your mother warns you about, but I did not care. After months of enforced celibacy, any woman was welcome, and I watched them with hungry eyes and lust burning through my body.

"Ahoy! James!" Peter waved over a large, red-bearded man. "Come and meet my new friend! This is James Kelly, William!"

The red-bearded man pushed through the crowd, smiling to me. "And who might you be, stranger?"

"William Sharpe," I said at once.

"That's a name as good as any other," Kelly said with a knowing smile. "Welcome to the Boston, my very own haven from the perils of sea and land."

"William's a veteran of the War," Peter said. "A cavalryman, no less."

"A cavalryman is it?" Kelly looked impressed. "We don't get many cavalrymen in here. Mostly sea-tramps, as you can see." He gave a little bow. "We are honoured with your presence, Trooper Sharpe."

"William is looking for a berth for the night," Peter said, "and maybe a willing woman."

"You've come to the right place, my man!" Kelly said. "You can stay here, and welcome." He looked around his bar. "What kind of girl do you prefer?"

I had never been asked that question before, and I am sure I stared at the man. "A female girl," I said, attempting humour.

"Redhead? Blonde? Brunette? Indian?" Kelly pointed out a woman of each description.

"Blonde," I said, for in truth I had been admiring the curves of a plump blonde ever since I stepped in the bar.

"An excellent choice," Kelly said. "We can settle the bill in the morning." He raised his voice above the commotion in the bar. "Nelly! There's a handsome man here looking for company. Make him happy!"

Nelly was a bouncy, willing companion. Within a few moments, she and I were seated together. Nelly was comfortable on my knee with her arms wrapped around my neck. Peter joined me, holding a red-headed virago as though his life depended on it, and other men joined us, with or without a female companion. After months of solitude, so much jollity was overwhelming, but Nelly had ways of cheering me up, and with her breasts pressed against me, and her hands busy elsewhere, I joined in the singing and drinking. That evening remains with me still – the laughter, the friendship and the free-flowing whiskey and rum. Peter and a large, bald man tried to teach me the words of a sea shanty when I realised the room was beginning to spin around me.

"That whiskey sure is powerful," I said.

Peter's grin seemed to expand until it spread all around his face. He became one huge grin, all teeth and a flapping pink tongue.

"William," Nelly pushed her face close to mine. I could see my reflection in her eyes, slightly hazy, yet still undoubtedly me. "There's a room upstairs. I've never had a black man before."

"Then you are in for a big surprise," I said, smiling.

"I'll carry your rifle," Nelly said. "You'll need a different weapon upstairs."

My friends laughed at that, adding humorously obscene comments. I lurched to my feet, swaying as I tried to balance so that Nelly had to help me out of that bar and up a flight of stairs. The stairs were carpeted, as I remember, with pictures of ships adorning the walls. The upper floor had a small corridor with rooms off, and Nelly guided me into one.

The bed was soft, and I sank down and down, with Nelly on top. "Let's get these clothes off you," she said and set to work as I lay there. "Here, have another drink." She poured more whiskey into my unresisting mouth, and the room span faster and faster. I saw Kelly join us, nodding down at my naked body.

"How much?" Kelly asked.

"About $70," Nelly said, with a new tone of voice. "He has weapons as well, and an old pipe. Nothing of value."

"A drifter," Kelly said. "*Emma Louise* for him."

I wondered vaguely who Emma Louise was, and what Kelly was doing in my bedroom.

"Let him keep the pipe," Kelly said.

"He's still conscious," Nelly said and thrust the neck of a whiskey bottle halfway down my throat. I swallowed to prevent myself from choking, and spun into a dark hole, down and down and down forever.

To this day, I do not know how long I was unconscious. It might have been one night, and it might have been a week. I opened my eyes with the worst headache I have ever experienced. I thought I was back in that hellish field hospital at Petersburg, except everything was dark, the whole world was moving, and a foul stench filled the air.

"He's awake at last!" A formidable voice said, adding a string of oaths for emphasis. "Get on your feet, you lazy lubber!"

I closed my eyes, unable to bear the pain in my head. A second later, somebody upended me. I fell to the floor with a mighty clatter, roared in pain, and yelled again as somebody landed a powerful blow across my backside.

"Get up, you lazy bastard! We've no space for passengers!"

"What the blue hell?" I shouted and tried to rise. I opened my eyes to see two men standing over me. One was my friend, Peter Hayes, holding a short length of rope; the other was a wiry, evil-eyed man I had never seen before.

"Get up, you lazy bastard!" Peter lifted his rope and whipped me across the chest.

I yelled again and forced myself to stand. I was in a tiny, dark room that swayed and bucked, with a single smoky lantern providing only dim light. I was also stark naked.

"Where am I?" The room was bucking crazily beneath me. "What's happened, Peter?"

"You're at sea, you dozy lubber!" Peter pushed me towards a low door and kicked me, hard, on my backside. "Now get on deck!"

On deck? I stared, realizing that my stocky friend was now my tormentor. "Am I on a ship?"

"Where the hell do you think you are?" Peter got busy with his rope's end again, and I forced myself up a vertical ladder and into the keenest wind I had ever known. Perhaps it was because I was naked, or the contrast between the fug down below and the howling wind on deck, but I thought I would freeze to death in my first few moments on that hell ship.

I could not keep my feet on the heeling deck, as four of us, all naked as new-born children, huddled in a group while Peter Hayes glowered at us with his rope's end in his hand.

"You green men better larn quick," he said, in an accent that was now all Down East. "You don't know the difference between water and tears. Well, I'll larn you." He stopped to stare at us. "Look at you! Not a stitch of clothing! You can't work like that!"

He sold us coarse canvas clothing from the ship's slop chest at prices that would raise a gasp in any big city, told us the cost would come from our wages, once we had worked off what it cost him to buy us from the boarding master, James Kelly. I did not understand much of what he said. I only knew I was suffering.

"Bully Hayes shanghaied you," a weather-worn seaman looked me up and down. "You look like you're used to an outdoor life, so it won't be as bad as you think."

"What?" I shook my head, still bewildered. "What do you mean?"

"James Kelly or Shanghai Kelly owns the Boston House. He's a notorious crimp, a man who gets seamen for undermanned ships. He kidnaps fools like you and sends them to sea. He owns half a dozen boarding houses and bars around the city."

I looked around at nothing. Outside the ship there was only the sea, always moving and wilder than I had ever thought possible. "It's a mistake. I'm not a sailor."

The seaman grunted. We were in the foc'sle, the sailor's word for the forecastle, the tiny, dark cabin where the crew slept. "You will be before this trip is over. You'll be a seaman, or you'll be dead." He held out his hand. "I'm Maxwell, by the way."

"William Sharpe." His hand was as hard as teak.

"This is yours, I believe," Maxwell handed over William's pipe.

I could feel the tears in my eyes as I held that pipe. "Thank you," I said. The words were inadequate for my feelings.

Those first few days on board were among the worst I ever experienced, even including the assault on the Crater. They were worse than the plantation because then I had known nothing else but slavery. They were worse than my recruit days in the Army because then I was training to fight for freedom. I wished, oh, so fervently, that I had remained in the wilderness, alone with my thoughts and the great abyss of the sky. However, I had not. I was on a ship bound for God-knew-where and must make the best of a bad situation.

Peter Hayes, or Bully Hayes as the crew called him, was the mate, and his job was to make life hell for all on board. He was very good at his job. Together with the second mate, a man named Thatcher, and the bosun, a bald monster who called himself Heath, he ran us ragged from dawn to dusk and from dusk to dawn.

Hayes had a particular dislike for a youngster named Jenkins and treated him even worse than he treated me. As a black man, I expected worse treatment, but Jenkins saved me from that experience on this ship.

As the days passed, I learned what had happened to me. Hayes and his bully mates toured the streets of Frisco, searching for men like me. They lured me to one of Shanghai Kelly's bars, where I was drugged with opium-laced whiskey and transported to ship.

Kelly made money from every man he shanghaied, sometimes up to three month's advance wages, plus what he could steal from our pockets. In my case, the captain also sold us cheap nautical clothing at shipboard prices, which were four times more than any shore-side shop. Crimping, as such practices were known, was a common factor in most US ports, with Frisco and New York particularly notorious. With no nautical skills, Bully Hayes made me work at the most menial of tasks.

"Who's the captain?" I asked in a rare moment between sweated labour.

"Captain Douglass," Maxwell whispered. "He was convicted of cruelty years ago and retired from the sea." He paused. "Officially."

I said nothing. I had no more energy to speak. Some of the crew recited a poem to me.

> *"Our captain is a tyrant*
> *The Bosun is a Turk*
> *The first mate is a bastard with the middle name of work."*

I worked. Together with the other men on that ship, I worked. Lord, how we worked. About half the crew were green, with Shanghai Kelly recruiting them the same way he had me, and after a week, Jenkins rebelled. He was a Welshman, a red-headed man with more courage than I had. Jenkins had come to California in the hope of digging gold, only to find himself captured even before he left Frisco. After days of Hayes' bullying, he rose in rebellion and challenged Hayes and Bosun Heath.

Hayes did not hesitate. The moment the Welshman lifted his fist, Hayes cracked him across the head with a steel marlinespike. Jenkins fell with a groan, and Hayes kicked him savagely in the ribs. I saw the blood seeping from Jenkins's head as Hayes kicked again, with the sound of splintering bone clearly audible.

"We should do something," I said to Maxwell.

"We should keep our heads down and say nothing," Maxwell whispered.

As Jenkins lay, moaning and semi-conscious on the deck, Hayes and Heath lifted him by his shoulders and feet, carried him to the bulwark and threw him into the sea.

"That's murder," I said. I had not seen anything like that in the US cavalry and had not expected to see it on an American ship.

The green men watched, too shocked to interfere. Only when the splash subsided, and the Welshman's body disappeared into the depths, did we move forward, and then it was too late. Thatcher, the second mate, stood at the mainmast with a revolver in his fist, staring at us.

That was the first time I saw the Captain. He appeared on the poop, wearing a smart blue uniform and with a smart blue cap on his head, adorned with gold braid, as if he was admiral of the US Navy rather than just the skipper of a battered old tub.

"What you saw was justice," Captain Douglass said in a cracked tone. "Remember the rule at sea. All the officers tell you to do is your duty. All you refuse to do is mutiny. The reward for mutiny is death."

We stared at this man who held our liberty and lives in his hands. He gave one last, long, sweeping look then retired to his cabin. After that display, we barely saw Captain Douglass, while the mates and the bosun carried revolvers wherever they were. The hazing continued, with Hayes as free with his rope's end as before and the ship heading south.

On that voyage, I learned a little bit of sailoring and a lot about American blood boats. American ships were notorious in every port in the world for their harsh treatment of the crew and sparkling appearance. British ships were infamous for starvation rations, Scandinavian vessels for efficiency, French for their easy-going ways and ours, Americans, for shining decks and a rule of fear. Hayes was the worst on our ship, a raging, ranting, unpredictable monster who could lay into a man with a rope's end one minute and act nearly human the next. The other officers, the second mate and the bosun, were almost as bad.

On the few occasions we saw the captain, he appeared on the poop, looked over the ship, checked aloft, barked instructions to Hayes and disappeared back into his cabin. From time to time, I saw empty bottles floating in our wake, to sink into the ocean. I was now in a different kind of hell. The plantation remained my benchmark of horror, but this was as bad in a different way. The army added the possibility of mutilation or death, while service with the 9th Cavalry carried the fear of slow torture. Now, I was a slave again. We were trapped in a ship, subject to the whims of a collection of mad tyrants, with the surrounding sea a more effective prison than stone walls or iron bars. There was not a single day when Bully Hayes did not lash me with a rope's end, or Thatcher punch or kick me. Life was a torment, and my body a mass of bruises before that first week was over.

"Endure," Maxwell advised. "Endure. Nothing lasts forever."

After one particularly bad day, I lay in my damp bunk, wondering if I should throw myself over the side for the fish when I fingered William's pipe. What would William say? "When we're home in Africa," William would say, "we will laugh at this, and tell tall stories to our grandchildren."

When we're home in Africa. I shook my head. My dream was further from realisation than it had ever been.

It was ten days before I even learned the name of the ship I was on.

"*Emma Louise*," Maxwell told me when I asked him. "She's a three-masted barquentine, and we're bound for New York with a mixed cargo." He bit on a wad of tobacco and began to chew. "We're going around Cape Stiff. The big H."

Maxwell waited for me to respond. He was what they called an Old Salt, with brass rings in both ears and faded tattoos on both arms. I think he had a wife somewhere, but in what port, I never learned. He was bound to sail the seas until he died, a man of the ocean who owed allegiance only to whatever ship he happened to be aboard. Maxwell had taken me under his wing and tried to teach me the rudiments of sailoring.

"Cape Stiff?" I did not know the name.

Maxwell favoured me with a gap-toothed grin. "There are

three Cape Stiffs," he told me, "and all are the devil's playground."

I listened with interest for I thought I had met the worst the devil could do with the tortures of the Apaches in Texas.

"One Cape Stiff is Guardafui on the Horn of Africa."

"Africa?" My interest increased. I had an immediate idea to jump off this ship off Africa and swim ashore.

Maxwell nodded as if he could read my mind. "You don't want to go ashore at Guardafui," he said. "The Horn of Africa is home to savage tribes, savage deserts and fanatical Muslims."

The chaplain of the 9th had taught us about Muslims. I did not know there were any in Africa. The chaplain had done his best to teach me, but now I began to realize how little I knew. I resolved to ask Maxwell to teach me about Geography. In the following weeks, he told me about the European powers and the British Royal Navy as well as increasing my knowledge of world geography.

In the meantime, Maxwell only told me about the three Cape Stiffs.

"The second Cape Stiff is also in Africa," Maxwell said. "It's in South Africa, the southern tip of the continent. Its official name is the Cape of Good Hope, but some sailormen call it the Cape of Storms."

"Is it stormy?" I had to ask.

"It can be," Maxwell said. "If a Cape Buster comes – that's the local storm – it will be as stormy as anywhere on the five oceans." He smiled. "The city at the Cape, Cape Town, is also called the Tavern of the Seas."

"Is it a black city?" I asked, hopefully.

"No," Maxwell shook his head. "It was Dutch, and now it's British, although much of the population is black."

"Do black people own any cities in Africa?"

"Black Muslims do," Maxwell said. "Cities in the desert. I think there are some black towns in West Africa, but you would not like to go there."

"Why not?" I asked.

"The area is bad for slavery, human sacrifice and that sort of thing," Maxwell said.

"I thought that had finished."

"It still exists in parts of Africa," Maxwell said. "The Muslim parts and some of the native kingdoms."

I hid my disappointment.

"The third Cape Stiff is the most terrible of them all," Maxwell said. "Cape Horn is at the southernmost tip of South America. In bad weather, it is a seaman's worst nightmare."

I had lost interest in stiff capes. I was thinking of Africa and slavery, for I had thought that only white men made us into slaves. I had not known that blacks also enslaved blacks in our own continent. The thought saddened me more than I can write.

I ROUND CAPE HORN

*M*axwell was not exaggerating about Cape Horn. *Emma Louise* came to the cape at the same time as what Maxwell described as a Cape Horn Snorter, which was another word for a storm. Despite my lack of experience, even I could feel that the ship was troubled, days before the storm hit. She lay sullen in glassy seas, rising and falling with sickening regularity as her masts spiralled against a low grey sky.

"We're in for the devil of a blow," Maxwell warned as Captain Douglass appeared on deck with a bottle in his hand and a curse on his lips.

"Trim these blasted sails, Mr Hayes, damn you for a landbound lubber," Douglass shouted. "Can't you feel the wind coming? It'll blow the canvas out of the gaskets, else!"

As Hayes sent the hands aloft, cursing and blinding, flogging the laggards with his ever-present rope's end, the wind increased. I was on deck, scrubbing the pine, and felt the fresh breeze turn to a gale within twenty minutes, and then mount to a storm. I thought I had seen all the extremes of weather in the brush country of Texas, but I was wrong. Until you have seen a Cape Horn storm, you have not experienced the worst that nature can create.

I had never seen, nor imagined, waves of the size and power that *Emma Louise* faced as she approached the Horn. The waves were like grey-blue mountains, shifting, moving, growling as they rose higher and higher, towering above our masts. We wallowed in the trough, and then rose to the crest of those waves, sharing the peak with curling greybeards and white spume so heavy it was like mist. Up there, when the wind blasted away the spindrift, we had a view of the ultimate waste, mile after mile of grey waves, stretching to infinity; it was a vista that chilled the blood and challenged the imagination.

Down there at the bottom of the world, with nothing but the iron-grey sea under an iron-grey sky, boys became men and men turned into screaming wrecks through fear. On one occasion, the helmsman shrieked in fear at the sight of the monstrous horror that reared up astern. He dropped his hold of the wheel and ran forward to the false security of the foc'sle. I saw him burrow under his bunk, shaking in terror, with his eyes wide and drool slithering from the corner of his mouth.

"Take that man's place!" Captain Douglass ordered. The captain had taken his place on the poop and remained there, lashed to the mizzen mast, day after day. That was the best I had seen him, and his presence reassured me, for however tired he looked, he did not abandon his post.

Maxwell took the helmsman's place, standing four-square with his feet planted on the deck and the wheel in his bronzed, capable hands. He chewed on a quid of tobacco as *Emma Louise* bucked and reared, span and gyrated, dancing to the tune of the storm.

I appreciated the seamanship of Douglass and the mates then, and the iron discipline they had installed in the crew. I did not like them any better, but I could understand why they had done what had to be done. It took more than ordinary courage to go aloft with such a sea running, and if fear helped drive the men onto the yardarms to furl the main royals, then Douglass and his bullies were expert at installing it.

Worst of all was the noise of the wind. I had never thought of wind as being an enemy, except the twisters of the prairies. Down there, at the southernmost ends of the earth, the wind dominated. That terrible Southern Ocean was the home of the wind, and it resented any intrusion by puny humans and their matchstick ships. Sometimes the wind screamed like a pig being slaughtered, sometimes it roared like a lion, and always it was the enemy. The wind tried to pluck the seamen from their perches on the yards, it threw countless tons of water at our hull, water that poured into the fo'csle, so we were huddled up to our knees or waist in bitter-cold water. The wind battered our senses, shrieking in our ears like a man under Apache torture, numbing our brains, throwing us around the ship. It lifted Charlie Dawson, a greenhorn shanghaied along with me; it ripped him bodily from the deck, suspended him in mid-air and dropped him back onto the solid pine. Just when we thought Charlie had a reprieve, a wave washed him to the rail, where he hung, shrieking, begging for our help until the wind tore his grasp free and tossed him into the waves. I saw him for a last, despairing instant, and then he was gone.

Every one of us suffered from the wind. Some had broken arms or ribs, we all carried cuts and bruises, but the worst damage was to our minds.

I will never forget that Cape Horn wind. It was malevolent, evil; it invaded all our senses. I think it was the voice of the devil himself, more terrifying than anything I had heard before. If I close my eyes now, I can hear it still, straining to sink *Emma Louise* and drown me in the terrible seas off Cape Stiff.

I could not say how long we fought Cape Horn. It was weeks rather than days, or it may even have been months. After a while, we knew nothing more than hissing, grey-bearded waves and the shrieking of the wind. Our lives shrunk into the fo'csle, the deck and the yards. Nothing mattered outside our little wooden world. Only survival mattered.

The Horn took three of our crew. Charlie Dawson, I have

already mentioned. The second was another first-voyager like myself. Maxwell taught us the old maxim "one hand for yourself and one for the ship," but sometimes we needed two hands for ourselves. I saw the wave coming from far astern, a foaming monster, twice as tall as our mainmast. *Emma Louise*, game as ever, lifted her stern to the water, higher and higher until it seemed that she would topple end over end. I swear that our bowsprit poked into the water forward before *Emma* started to right herself. The first voyager, a swarthy Mexican, turned around to face the wave, opened his mouth in a scream, and then the wave hit.

With Maxwell at the helm, we were as safe as any vessel in such conditions. However, the Mexican panicked and the sea took him. I stretched out my hand in a pointless attempt to catch him as the wave swept him along the deck. I can still see his eyes as he realised he was going to die. Such hopeless despair I never want to see again. The sea brushed him forward, smashed him against the foremast, then carried him out of our sight. The Mexican vanished as if he had never existed, and I cannot even remember his name.

Our third and final loss was more important to the ship than the other two combined. Bully Hayes was one of the most unpleasant men I have ever met, a slave driver of the most repugnant kind. Yet, for all that I could say against him, and that is plenty, he was a superb seaman. With the loss of Bully Hayes, some of the soul left the ship. He was aloft, splicing a line as *Emma Louise* bounced like a cork. Such antics did not concern the Bully, who was as sure-footed aloft as a normal man in a city street. I do not know how the footrope snapped. Perhaps it was rotted with seawater, or just old, although one of the crew swore he saw a spectre of Charlie Dawson saw the rope with a knife, and he may well have been correct. Bully Hayes grabbed hold of the yard when the footrope snapped, and he hung there with his hands slowly sliding from the wet, slippery wood. He made no noise, neither calling for help nor cursing his luck. I watched as the mate fell, still wordless, to land in the sea. He sank at once as if the sea welcomed him home, and he never surfaced again. He's in Davy Jones's Locker now, tormenting poor damned seamen and bullying the mermaids and killer sharks, God rot his evil heart.

When it claimed Bully Hayes, the storm decided it had completed its work. Immediately the mate drowned; the sea began to moderate. As Maxwell told me later, we had been half a league south of Staten Island at the southernmost point of our journey and steered our bow north. I have never been as far south before and hope to God never to return.

Emma Louise sailed north. We had rounded Cape Horn and sailed into the South Atlantic. Maxwell was not alone in thinking we should call at Port Stanley in the Falkland Islands for minor repairs and replenish our water.

"Damn the Falklands," Captain Douglass growled, once more resorting to the bottle. "The Limeys are there, and I'm damned if I'll drink their water."

So we sailed past the Falkland Islands because it was British, and the crew growled that they needed a run ashore.

"Keep the men working, Mister Thatcher! There's no excuse for slacking! A good dose of the rope's end is what they need!"

Yet without Hayes, *Emma Louise* was a quieter ship. Thatcher and Heath tried their best to reimpose their reign of terror, but with less success. After Cape Horn, the greenhorns were seasoned mariners and harder to cow with hard work and the sting of a rope. The Cape had taken its dues and, in return, had put steel into the crew. We sailed north, with *Emma Louise* making good progress for another week, and then the wind lessened, day by day.

"Now the trouble starts," Maxwell predicted as we hung over the bulwark amidships.

"Trouble?" I looked at him. "I thought we left the trouble behind at the Horn."

"Have you noticed how the wind has dropped?" Maxwell said, chewing his tobacco.

"I have," I said. "It makes for very pleasant sailing."

Maxwell spat into what remained of the wind. "The wind's dying," he said. "We're heading into a dead calm, and by the look of the sea and the sky, it will last for days."

I did not understand the implications until the wind disappeared the next day. We lay becalmed on a sea like liquid glass, with the reflection of *Emma Louise* our mirror-image under a sky of brass. Captain Douglass appeared on the poop again, ordering Thatcher and Heath to keep the ship moving. They tried; they sent the hands clambering up the rigging to throw water on the sails to catch even a breath of wind. When that attempt failed, they launched the gig and the dinghy – the ship's boats – and ordered the men to tow *Emma Louise*. I was in the gig beside Maxwell, who gave quiet instructions to those of us who had never rowed before. To an observer, rowing looks easy, but I found it harder than fieldwork in the plantation, pulling on the oars under a burning sun. For all the sweat we expended in that stinking boat, we could not see any progress as *Emma Louise* crawled forward, inch by inch.

"Don't worry, boys," Didcot, a bald-headed man who made a practice of complaining, said. "Only another eight thousand miles to go."

"Keep busy," Maxwell told me. "Idleness is the curse of the sailor and the mother of mutiny."

As always, Maxwell was correct. During the next few days, as the wind refused to blow, *Emma Louise* floundered. With the ship's sails limp and the sea flat to the iron bar of the horizon, the crew's grumbling increased. The men voiced their resentment at the early days of hazing and the death of Jenkins and swore belated violence on Heath and Thatcher. I remembered the mutinies in the 9th Cavalry, the murder of an unpopular officer and the wasted lives of two good men. I said nothing, kept my head down and prayed for a wind that never came.

The subdued mutterings rose to grumblings and then small, sneaky acts of violence. As men encouraged each other, the disobedience grew bolder. Somebody climbed aloft, waited until the bosun was on deck, and dropped a marlinespike, which missed by a few inches. Next night, an anonymous voice threatened revenge on the second mate, and somebody threw a bottle aft from the foc'sle.

"Keep out of it," Maxwell warned me. "Don't take sides and clamp your teeth together. Nobody wins in a mutiny."

Captain Douglass appeared on the poop again, talking quietly to Thatcher and Heath, with all three openly carrying revolvers. That night, as the crew sweated in the stuffy foc'sle, I heard rumblings on deck.

"Lie still," Maxwell advised. "Ride out the storm."

Next morning I saw the officer's retaliation. During the night they had rolled the waters barrels aft and now held them under armed guard.

"We don't know when we'll see land again," Maxwell reminded. "Water is more precious than gold dust." He shook his head. "We should have stopped at the Falklands to replenish our water barrels, so damn Captain Douglass and his stiff Yankee pride!"

Thatcher placed a water keg right aft and hoisted it up the mizzen, so anybody wishing a drink had to climb aloft. *Emma Louise* was a divided ship, with the officers controlling the aft half and the hands the forward. All the time, we wallowed on an empty sea, with no sail to break the unrelenting bar of the horizon and the sun pouring its heat on the suffering *Emma Louise*.

In the foc'sle, men spoke openly of rushing aft and taking over the ship.

"How many of you can navigate?" Maxwell asked, without leaving his bunk.

The resulting silence answered his question.

"Nor can I," Maxwell said. "We can't change what's happened, and mutiny will only make things worse. You've made your protest, now keep quiet and pray for wind and a smooth passage to New York. You can complain to the police there, for all the good it will do." He settled back into his straw donkey-mattress, closed his eyes and tried to sleep. I joined him.

With no wind, there was little work aloft, and Captain Douglass tried to keep us busy scrubbing the already immaculate decks, painting the hull and checking the cargo. All the time, the water keg hung above the deck, tempting us with its proximity.

Not surprisingly, it was the water situation that provided the final stimulus for mutiny. After a few days, the water aloft turned green and slimy, with a thin scum forming on top. Another day of thirst and we noticed living things moving inside the water, horrible, wriggling little creatures like white worms. The grumbles increased.

"Tomorrow," Maxwell mouthed to me. "Keep your head down until all the noise and fury blow over. Don't get involved, whatever happens." He gave me a nod and settled down, with his eyes closed.

I lay down, held William's pipe and told myself things would be better when we were home in Africa. At that moment, I was not thinking about Africa. I was wishing I had remained alone in the wilderness of the American Southwest. I understood things there, while out at sea, nothing made sense to me.

A mutiny at sea is something I never want to experience again. At my age, it is unlikely that I will, thank the Lord.

The trouble began with the rising of the sun. Sunrise in the Doldrums is nearly as spectacular as in the Arizona desert. I stared at the dawn, with the sea a liquid gold ball rising from a corn-coloured sea and the horizon flat as a ruler and empty as a harlot's heart. Nature always enthralled me with its beauty, from the intricacy of the smallest flower to the majesty of a desert sierra, and this sunrise was one of the finest sights a man can see.

"Now!" The call came from behind me. I stepped aside as four of the crew exploded from the foc'sle and charged aft, with bald-headed Didcot to the fore. I did not know what they planned, and groaned inwardly, knowing that nothing good would come of it. I heard the crack of a revolver and saw one of the crew fall. Jackson, it was, a rather simple-minded man from Connecticut, a follower who believed the last thing that anybody told him. Rather than quell the outbreak, the shot seemed to encourage the men, with three others rushing aft. Bored, thirsty, resentful men are not easily intimidated.

They jumped over Jackson as he lay writhing, with his blood staining the deck I had spent so many hours scrubbing.

Maxwell sighed. "I wasn't going to get involved," he said, chewing mightily on his tobacco. "It looks like I'm going to have to, now."

"On whose side?" I asked.

"The officers," Maxwell said. "These fools look set to kill us all. Without a navigator, we'll drift forever in the ocean. Are you with me?"

I thought of the nightmare of the early days on board *Emma Louise* and closed my mind. I had no desire to help slave drivers. Being a slave cast a long shadow, even darkening my common sense.

"No," I said.

As soon as I spoke, Maxwell moved, running aft to help restore order. I watched from the lee of the foremast, forgetting about the beauty of the dawn in the drama of the moment. Yet even as *Emma Louise* became a ship of more violence, a thousand memories crammed into my head. I had travelled a hard trail from the old plantation days, to a Union infantryman, a Buffalo Soldier, a wanderer and now a sailor. Would my adventures end with me dying of thirst in a drifting ship in the middle of the South Atlantic?

"We'll laugh at this when we're home in Africa," William whispered in my ear. "Don't desert your friend."

The revolver cracked again. I saw another man fall, thought for a second that it was Maxwell, and breathed again when I saw him silhouetted against the taffrail. Maxwell lifted his hands to try to stop the trouble. I watched, uncertain what to do, unwilling to help men who had driven me like a slave, but hoping Maxwell was not hurt. The second shooting infuriated the crew further; they fell on the mate and bosun with all their pent-up frustration.

"Stop!" Maxwell roared. "If you kill these men, you are killing yourselves." He was too late to save Heath. The crowd fell upon him in a frenzy. The bosun fought, swinging a marlinespike like a man demented, yelling with a mixture of fear and anger. The crew knocked him to the deck, surrounded him, kicked him stupids and threw him overboard. I saw him try to clamber up the side of the ship, only for Didcot to crash a marlinespike onto his hands, sending him back into the water.

"Drown you bastard!" Didcot shouted.

At that point, Captain Douglass appeared on the poop with a revolver in his hand. He fired in the air, with the noise momentarily quelling the riot.

"I'll shoot the next man to move, by God!" Captain Douglass lowered his aim.

"Will you now?" Didcot said, scooping up the revolver Heath had dropped. As the captain swivelled, Didcot fired. His first bullet hit the rail at Douglsass's side, the second hit the captain in the shoulder, spinning him around. He fired back, missing, and the crew surged to the poop, marlinespikes and boots flying. Somebody lifted the captain's revolver and shot him again, and again.

"Over the side with him!"

Douglass joined Heath in the sea, floated for a moment with the blood seeping from him, and disappeared with a swirl as a shark took him.

"Stop there," Maxwell strode into the mob, pushing the crew away from Thatcher. "We need this man alive."

Maxwell was too late. The crew remembered the days of bullying and wanted blood, Thatcher's blood. Maxwell stepped in again, pulling at the men, trying to save Thatcher's life.

"Don't kill him," Maxwell pleaded. "We need him!"

"Whose side are you on?" Didcot asked

"Everybody's," Maxwell said.

"Did you hear that?" Didcot shouted. "Max is supporting Thatcher! He's on their side."

A few of the crew turned around, still with the lust for violence in their eyes. "We'll see to Max later," Schmidt, a scar-faced man promised.

"Max!" I stepped to his side. "I don't think they're listening." I saw the flash of a knife and heard a terrible scream.

"He won't make any more babies," Schmidt grunted, and other men laughed, hysterically. Another knife flickered, plunging down again and again. I saw the blood spread across the deck.

"That's the mate gone," I said. "Come on, Max, we'll let the boys calm down."

The crew did not calm down. They killed off the second mate, threw the body overboard and came after Maxwell, spreading out across the deck. Schmidt left bloody footsteps as he walked.

"Get away from me, William," Maxwell said. "They're going to kill me," he sounded remarkably calm for a man about to die. "There's no need for you to suffer as well."

I took a deep breath, stamped my feet on the deck and thought of William. "No," I said, "we'll stand together."

When the crew saw us standing resolute, they hesitated, and these few moments probably saved our lives. I clenched my fists, spread my feet for balance and waited.

"Look!" I pointed to the sails. "The wind is back!"

The topsail ruffled first, and then the mainsail. It started with a faint waver on the canvas, then a few moments later, the topsail began to belly, pushing *Emma Louise* forward for the first time in weeks.

"We're moving," Didcot shouted. "We're moving again, boys. Douglass was a Jonah! New York, here we come!"

In the excitement of finding the wind, the crew temporarily forgot about us. Didcot ran into the captain's cabin to break open Douglass's private spirit store and returned on deck with a bottle of Kentucky Rye in each hand. "See what I've found, boys! Time to celebrate freedom from tyranny!"

Within an hour, *Emma Louise* bounded forward with all sails drawing, and nobody at the wheel as most of her crew sprawled drunk on deck.

"Captain Douglass must have had an extensive supply of whiskey," I said.

"It seems so," Maxwell said. "I'm leaving, Will." Maxwell had not touched the drink. I think we were the only sober men on board that ship.

"Leaving?" I glanced around at the sea. The sun had set, and stars formed an arc of lights in the dark sky, while a crescent moon glowed softly upon us. "We're in the middle of the ocean. Where can you go?"

"Anywhere except here," Maxwell gestured to the ship's boats. "I'll take the gig and get away as quickly as possible. When that rabble," he jerked a contemptuous thumb towards the crew, "when that rabble sobers up, they'll remember my attempts to save Thatcher." Maxwell gave a sour grin. "This ship is doomed, Will. If they manage to reach a port, they'll be hanged for murder, mutiny and piracy."

I had not considered that. If I was arrested, the authorities might also discover my past and hang me for murder as well. As a black deserter in front of a white American jury, I did not expect mercy to tinge justice. I could already feel the hempen noose rough around my throat.

"Can I come with you?" I asked.

I AM ADRIFT

"*I*'ve no plan," Maxwell said. "We might find land, and we might not. We might starve to death, or die of thirst, or drown."

I nodded. "I'll take the chance."

Maxwell nodded. "We'll head eastwards and hope to hit land, or mebbe a ship will find us and pick us up. Are you with me?"

"I'm with you," I said.

We collected as much water and food as we could, stepping carefully over the sprawling drunken wreckage on deck, and carried our supplies to the gig. Maxwell found a compass and charts in the captain's cabin, and we lowered the gig into the now-choppy sea and pushed off, eastward.

"Would we not be better heading west?" I asked. "Sail towards the Americas? Then we could get back to the States."

"See this chart?" Maxwell showed me the chart he had rescued from the captain's cabin. "That X is the last position Douglass marked. We must have drifted eastward when we were in the Doldrums. We're about five hundred miles nearer to Africa than the Americas by my reckoning, and anyway, the wind's coming from the west. If it holds, we might hit land in a week or so. If it holds."

"And if it doesn't hold?" I asked.

"Then we pray," Maxwell said.

"I've never had much luck with prayer," I said.

"Nor have I," Maxwell gave a crooked smile. "Anyway, if we arrive in America, the local sheriff will probably hang us. I don't fancy that."

I nodded. "Eastwards it is." It was not until we hoisted the sail that I realised what was happening. I was going to Africa.

"We'll laugh at this later," I said to William, as I fingered his pipe. "When we're home in Africa."

"What was that?" Maxwell asked.

"I said, we'll soon be home in Africa."

The wind held. I watched *Emma Louise* sink slowly away, with her sails pushing her north-west into the waste of the South Atlantic, as we angled our single lateen sail and let the wind take us where it willed.

Dawn found us alone on a silver-blue sea, with no sign of *Emma Louise* and a pleasant breeze skiffing white spray from the top of the waves.

"I had hoped to see another sail," Maxwell confessed. "We must be crossing at least one shipping lane."

We did not see another sail. From our small boat, the horizon was much more limited, and the waves higher, but without the menace of the Cape Horn growlers. We bowled along, making good time as Maxwell consulted his compass, estimated our position on the chart and checked the sky. "It looks like the weather will hold," he said.

That was the first time I enjoyed being at sea, with the sun warm, the air crisp and no bully mates to harass me. I had only a cross on the chart to tell me where I was, no thought for the future and sufficient food and water for my immediate needs. Only the present mattered and the flying fish that played around us.

"We're making good progress," I said.

"We are," Maxwell agreed.

We spoke then. Maxwell asked me about my life, and I told him about the plantation and the war, and life as a Buffalo Soldier. He listened, asked questions and understood when I was reticent.

"On board a ship," Maxwell told me, "we treat a man on his merits, not on his past. We don't care what he did yesterday, only how he acts in a storm, or how he shares with sailors who have less."

"Even though I'm black?" I asked.

Maxwell spat into the wind. "On a ship, you are a seaman first and anything else later. Our fight is with the sea and the wind, nothing else."

"Hayes and the rest did not act like that," I reminded.

"They are an anomaly," Maxwell said. "There is more democracy on a good ship than anywhere else."

I held onto Maxwell's words as the wind pushed us on, mile after mile, league after league, day after day. I asked Maxwell about his life, and he told me tales of China Sea pirates and the islands of the east. He told me of the massed shipping at London, the centre of world trade. He had seen the Royal Navy exercising in the Channel and the fever-ravaged anti-slavery patrols off West Africa. Maxwell gave me a rough idea of geography, of the oceans and continents of the world and where the United States fitted into the globe.

I listened, learned and wondered.

One day, a providential shower of rain provided drinking water to supplement the green slime which was all we had. We caught the rain in our sail, squeezed out the salt-spray, caught more rain and filled the kegs. We laughed as we worked, two men with vastly different experiences of life, one white, one black, but without racial differences, we were only two men together. We sat in a bobbing speck in a limitless sea, and I was happy.

On another day, two flying fish landed in the boat, providing us with some welcome fresh food.

"Can you eat raw fish?" Maxwell asked.

I found that I could. During my time wandering across America, I had eaten everything from rattlesnake to cactus. Raw fish was merely another strange food to try.

On the seventh or eighth day away from *Emma Louise*, the wind dropped, leaving us drifting on a limpid sea. With recent memories of the Doldrums, I suppressed a shiver. "What happens now?" I asked.

"We've sat here in comfort long enough," Maxwell said. "It's time for some exercise." He unshipped two pairs of oars, winked, and handed a pair to me. "You know what to do, and this time there's no ship to tow."

We took it steadily, pulling slowly towards the east, with Maxwell's compass pointing the way. For hour after hour, we bent, dipped, hauled and lifted, with the iron bar of the horizon seemingly immobile, inviolate, never receding, and never closing. We were rowing from nowhere to nowhere, and the world was all ocean. On the tenth day after we left *Emma Louise*, the sharks appeared. At first, we only saw one, with the sinister black triangle of the dorsal fin cutting through the water astern of us, waiting to feed.

"We have company," I said.

"Yes," Maxwell nodded, pulling with casual ease.

We kept rowing, trying to ignore the sharks. The second shark joined an hour later, and the third an hour after that. I say an hour, but that time is an approximation, for neither Maxwell nor I possessed a watch. Even the days began to merge now, one easing into another in a never-ending succession of dark following light, with a sky of brilliant stars then days of long horizons and increasing thirst. The evil dorsal fins remained with us.

I don't know how long we were in that open boat. Weeks, certainly, and it seemed as if the entire world contracted into that wooden clinker hull. The final few days were as bad as any I had experienced. Partially dehydrated, with thumping headaches, salt boils and blistered palms, we were hungry, thirsty and exhausted. Yet we still rowed, pulling by instinct, as if we had done nothing else all our lives.

"We're moving faster," Maxwell said, the first words he had uttered for hours. "We're caught in a current."

I did not argue. Lack of food and water, with constant exposure to the sun, had drained my strength. I continued to row, with my hands like claws and my salt-water boils merging until I was one immense pain.

"Land!" Maxwell said.

I could not think what Maxwell said. The word made no sense. There was no land; there was only the sea, hissing, moving, rising and falling, only the sea forever.

"Land," Maxwell repeated.

I looked up, still rowing, with my dazed, undernourished mind unable to comprehend the concept. I could see a long, hard line ahead, with a blue haze behind that might be distant mountains. It seemed a lifetime since I had seen mountains.

"Where are we?" I asked.

Maxwell looked as bad as I felt. "I don't know," he admitted. "I can only guess."

"Where do you guess we are?" I said.

"Somewhere off the coast of Africa," Maxwell said.

Africa. I felt for Will's long-stemmed pipe that I had carried all the way from Texas. "We've got to Africa, William. I've brought you home to Africa."

Maxwell looked at me from his sunburned face with the flaking lips and blisters. He did not say anything. I put the pipe away. William would understand.

"That's to the west," I said, looking at our compass. "Should Africa not be on the east?"

Maxwell nodded. "We must have passed the Cape and drifted up the east coast."

I stared at the stern bar to the west. Despite the enormous distances we had travelled on the empty ocean, the land still seemed to be very far away, a dream to torment us, rather than a tangible reality only a few miles distant. "Can we get there?" I asked.

"We can try," Maxwell said. "It all depends on the current and the tide."

We returned to the rowing, pointing the bow of the gig towards the land and putting steady effort into the work. We had to crane over our shoulders to check our progress. While I was staring towards the land, Maxwell was first to see the sail, and we both watched it in hope.

"Sail, ho!" Maxwell croaked.

"Ahoy," I said, with every word scratching my parched throat like broken glass.

Neither of us had the energy to raise a hand, and the ship did not see us. It sailed past, at least a mile distant, taking my hopes with it.

That was the first and only sail we had seen since we left *Emma Louise.*

I heard the rumble before Maxwell and wondered what it was. "That's like gunfire," I said, with memories of the cannon fire of the Civil War returning. I flinched involuntarily as if a Confederate cannon of some 12 years before could harm our little gig.

"It's not cannon fire," Maxwell said. "It's worse."

"Thunder?" I looked at the cloudless sky, dreading a sudden storm that might drive us back out to sea.

"Surf," Maxwell said. "That's surf crashing onto the shore."

"Is that bad?" I asked.

"If we can hear it a-way out here," Maxwell said, "it's bad. I've known boats overturned and their crews drowned in the surf."

We stopped rowing then as the tide caught us. After days and weeks of drifting and rowing, now we seemed to race towards the shore.

"Hold on," Maxwell said. "This is going to get rough."

I had lived all my life inland, and except for a brief look at the coast at Frisco, I had never seen the beach. My first view of Africa was a long, white band, accompanied by a sinister roar as the sea tried to pound the land into submission.

The roaring increased as we approached, and then the gig tilted sideways. I held onto the bulwark, swearing, felt the keel grind on something hard and held on tighter as we lifted again. My relief was short-lived as the surf foamed on either side of us, silver-white, and then we capsized. I felt myself thrown into the water, waved my hands helplessly, gulped salt water and tried to find the seabed with my feet. It seemed ironic to drown as we reached land, and then the wave lifted me and hammered me down on what seemed like an iron surface.

I lay there, gasping, for what seemed like hours, gagging as my lungs and throat burned. Waves broke around me, each one pushing me further up the beach until I lay beyond the furthest wave. Only then did the realization hit me. I was in Africa; William and I were home in Africa. I felt for William's pipe and panicked when I could not find it.

"Oh, God, no!" I raised my head, tried to rise and failed. The world spun around me.

"You're still alive then," Maxwell grabbed my shoulders and dragged me further up the beach.

"I am. So are you." I looked for the pipe. The beach was empty except for a couple of questing birds.

"Here," Maxwell thrust the pipe towards me. "You must have dropped this in the landing."

"Thank you." I held the pipe as if my life depended upon it, or my soul.

I AM IN AFRICA

*N*ow that I had arrived, I wished I knew more about this continent. I only knew what the chaplain of the 9th and Maxwell had taught me. I looked around, seeing a never-ending beach marked by high surf, with mountains inland. I saw what remained of our gig, a splintered wreck, with half the timber smashed. We had no way back and nowhere to go.

"Are you fit?" Maxwell asked me.

I nodded, although I had hardly been less fit in my life. Whatever happened, good or bad, my future lay in Africa.

"Then let's find water," Maxwell said.

We walked along the beach, putting one foot in front of the other, with all our strength concentrated on the necessity to keep moving. Sea birds screamed overhead, mocking us with their cries. We were shipwrecked mariners, and although some people may find that concept romantic, the reality is only pain, sick weariness and physical exhaustion.

We were very fortunate that we did not have far to go, or we would have died on that sunlit, terrible shore.

I became aware of a group of people watching me. Black faces and black bodies with little to cover them, they kept pace with us, talking to each other in a language utterly unknown to us. I tried to shout, but saltwater and fatigue had closed my throat.

"People," I croaked to Maxwell.

He looked up. "I see them." He lifted a hand in acknowledgement, and the group came closer, young women with wide eyes.

"Water," Maxwell said. "Do you have any water?"

They looked at each other, spoke together and ran away.

"Don't go," Maxwell pleaded.

I tried to follow, stumbled, and fell, face-first on the sand. I could have remained there, for it would have been easy to let sleep and death drift me away.

"Get up!" Maxwell pulled at my arm. "Live."

William was beside me, smiling. "When we're in Africa," he said, "we'll laugh at this."

I was in Africa, and I was not laughing.

I had no sooner regained my feet than the women appeared, this time with two men. They surrounded us, with one of the men holding a gourd.

"Water?" Maxwell asked, and the man beamed.

I have seldom seen a happier face. The stranger held the gourd out to Maxwell, who drank with long, hard swallows, then passed it to me. Nectar from the Gods could not have tasted better than that warm water, and I am sure I would have cried if I had sufficient moisture for tears.

The group surrounded us, laughing and all talking together, and took us around a point of sand to their village. A score of people congregated to see these strangers the sea had deposited on their doorstep.

The village was small and simple, of round, mud-and-thatch huts and poor, chattering people who seemed pleased to help all they could. They took us to an elderly man who must have been the local chief and who lived in a hut slightly larger than the rest.

The elderly man looked at us and spoke in a strange language before he tried in English.

"We're looking for a town," Maxwell said.

"Tomorrow," the old man said and waved us away. That was the only intelligible word he spoke to us, but he repeated it as often as he could. I think it was the only English word he knew, and he was very proud of his scholarship.

We spent three days and nights in that small, friendly village, and I don't think I have ever drunk more water in my life. The chief gave us a hut to ourselves, and various people left fish stew and some maize – or mealie, as we call it here – porridge that was very welcome.

Only when we felt sufficiently strong to continue did we move on, with half the village surrounding us, all excitedly talking as they tried to communicate their thoughts.

"Tomorrow," the chief said proudly, handing us each a gourd of water and a piece of dried fish.

"Tomorrow," we replied solemnly and shook his hand.

That was my introduction to Africa, and it could hardly have been better. I learned then that the ordinary African people were friendly and generous to strangers in need. Although I later met a great number of very aggressive and hostile Africans, I believe that my first impression was the true one, and only circumstances have created the violence.

We had barely walked an hour when we found the white man's civilization.

The town of East London could have been transported to Texas or California without raising an eyebrow. I knew at once that it was a frontier town, with the same mixture of white and native faces, a similar style of architecture and the same pulsating energy and feeling of nothing being completed. Only the presence of the sea was different, and the mass of round black faces. I tried to communicate with the black folk without success. I did not understand a word of their language, and their English seemed non-existent. Judging by their clothes and general demeanour, they were only labourers and in no better circumstances than the black population of the United States.

After a positive start with the tomorrow village, Africa was not what I had hoped, but it was early days yet.

With no money, we needed to find a job to eat. The generosity of the village was lacking in East London, as is the way of civilization. The more advanced and large the city, the less friendly and helpful the people, in my experience. Maxwell and I scrounged what we could, and then hunted for work. I think Max and I both knew that our paths would soon part, although neither of us spoke of the parting. We were different creatures that fate and the sea had thrown together, and that was all.

It was not easy to lower myself to the level of a labourer, and harder still when I did not know the local languages. However, the only other occupations that seemed open for black people was wagon-driving, a skill I lacked, or acting as a servant to a white man. I refused to call anybody master again.

"What do you plan?" I asked Maxwell as we sat on the waterfront among the scavenging birds, watching the river flow past.

"I'll find a ship," Maxwell said. "I'll go back to sea. It's all I know." He looked sideways at me. "You can come too, William. You've more experience than many, now, and I'll keep you from harm."

I seriously considered the idea. A seaman was a labourer afloat, and not all ships were as horrific as *Emma Louise*. Food, work and accommodation, and the friendship of Maxwell. It was tempting. "No," I said, with regrets, for I knew I would never see Max again. He was my second real friend. "No, I've been dreaming of Africa for years. I haven't given up on Africa, yet."

We shook hands and parted as friends. Such is the way of the sea. I often think of Maxwell, with the adventures we shared, and I wonder how he fared on the oceans of the world, always restless, never knowing a proper home. He called himself a sea-nomad, and that is what he was.

With my knowledge of English and maritime experience, I found a casual job in the harbour, rowing seamen and merchants out to their ships. Some called me Kaffir or worse terms, but they paid in coin and overall treated me better than they would have in Savannah or Charleston. Around the harbour, I listened to conversations, learned snippets of the local languages and gathered information about the area and what was happening.

Although much of this southern tip of Africa was under British control, there were large areas where the Union Flag did not wave. Similar to the United States, there was a mobile frontier, with native tribes and even nations who were reluctant to submit to British authority. When I learned some of the local words, I asked about any powerful African kingdoms I could perhaps join. The same answer came back. "Don't," they said. "The Galeka are unfriendly, the Amapondo treacherous, and the Matabele will kill you." They mentioned a dozen names, all unfamiliar to me. Apparently, most native chiefs would kill me out of hand. "The Basotho are the most civilised," they said, which sounded hopeful. They always mentioned one native kingdom with fear.

"Don't go near Zululand," everybody said.

While some of the white colonists treated me little better than a slave, the local blacks seemed only to work when under supervision and barely spoke English. What little I learned in those early weeks, I picked up from the Hottentots or Totties.

I did not like the Hottentots as a race. I thought them friendly on the surface and devious beneath, ready to promise the earth and deliver a handful of dirt. In my experience, they were untrustworthy. They seemed to look down on the black people and favour the whites. However, I learned that southern Africa was home to another white people who did not like the British. These people called themselves Boers, and both the Hottentots and blacks disliked them. I asked more about the independent black kingdoms.

"There are a few kingdoms beyond the frontiers," a woman

told me. She ran a small beer shop near the harbour, calling it an inn.

"Which frontiers?" I thought of my years guarding the Rio Grande and the Texas frontier.

"South Africa is a mess of frontiers." The woman called herself Ma Thomas and was a Cape Coloured, with a British soldier for a father and a Tottie as a mother. We spoke inside the small inn that she ran, with a scattering of customers entering and leaving. I was surprised that some white sailors were among her visitors, rubbing shoulders with the blacks in total equality.

"What sort of mess?" I asked.

"Look." Ma Thomas dipped her finger into a jug of beer and traced the outline of southern Africa on one of her three tables. "The British control the southernmost tip, the Cape Colony." She drew a wet line on the map to show the rough extent of British authority. "And they claim this part here, Natal." She indicated an area further up the east coast. "Between these areas of British control is the part they call Kaffirland or Kaffraria, which consists of independent black kingdoms. These are Xhosa tribes, with the Galekas the most powerful."

"I should go there," I said, looking into her disturbingly intelligent brown eyes. "I was a soldier," I said. "I'd like to fight for an independent black kingdom."

Ma Thomas gave me a sidelong look. "The British are gearing up for a war with the Galekas now," she said. "Before you decide to fight, maybe have a look at them. You have the bearing of a civilised man, and the Galeka, like all Xhosa, are savages."

I said nothing to that, for what I had seen of the black folk in Africa had not always impressed me. I had expected proud warriors and mainly found cringing labourers with the mentality of slaves.

"Inland of the British," Ma Thomas said, "there are the Boers, white men of Dutch extraction who don't like the British and treat the black people worse than they treat cattle."

My idea for joining a black kingdom seemed to disappear

when I learned of the situation here. "Are there any other native kingdoms?" I asked. "Civilised ones?"

"There are the Swazis," Ma Thomas said, "and the Basothos or Basutos; they are fairly civilised."

"The Zulus?" I asked, with my hope fading further.

"The Children of Heaven?" Ma Thomas shook her head. "King Cetswayo's people are the most powerful black kingdom in Africa, I believe, but civilised?" She shook her head. "If you mean like the civilization you know, then no, they are not civilised. They have a distinct culture." Ma Thomas tried to divert me. "The Matabele, further north, are also powerful."

I refused to be diverted. "Tell me more about the Zulus."

"Everybody is afraid of the Zulus," Ma Thomas said. "Even the Boers and the British treat them with respect."

I decided that I wanted to find out more about this independent black nation that even the mighty British respected. I was sure the Zulu king Cetswayo would welcome a veteran black soldier from America. But first, I wanted to see how the British fought. "You said there might be war with the Galekas?"

"I reckon so," Ma Thomas said. "They have begun raiding the farms of British settlers. The British will turn the other cheek for a while, and then they will retaliate, and the Galekas will lose more lands and more cattle."

"I might wander over to the Frontier," I said. "I used to be a soldier."

"You said that," Ma Thomas reminded. "Tell me more," she took hold of the sleeve of my jacket, "afterwards."

Ma Thomas did not have to tell me more. I have always liked women, and, in turn, I have always been able to please them. Ma Thomas had no complaints after she led me to her bed, and neither had I. She was older than me by at least ten years and had used at least some of that decade to perfect her skills with men. Ma Thomas knew more tricks than any of the harlots from the Texas bordellos, with the addition of genuine warmth. I could have remained with her for longer than the three weeks I was there.

We were both genuinely sad when I said farewell.

"Are you going off to war?" Ma Thomas asked.

"I am," I confirmed.

"You have neither a rifle nor a horse," Ma Thomas pointed out. "I can give you some money to buy them."

"That is a very generous offer," I said, quite moved.

"I'll fetch my purse." Ma Thomas stepped back inside the inn.

"No," I stopped her. "You've done enough for me. I'll find a horse on the way." After stealing from the Apaches, I did not foresee any difficulties in finding a horse in South Africa.

Ma Thomas nodded. "As you wish. Come back any time." She planted a wet kiss on my cheek. "My house and my bed are always open for you."

Ma Thomas stood in her doorway, watching as I walked away. When I turned back, a few moments later, full of doubts to leave such happiness behind, Ma Thomas was deep in conversation with a handsome young buck. I watched her slip a hand around his hips in a move I knew well, sighed, and resumed my journey. I had only been one man in her life that had been full of men, and she had been one woman in my life of plenty.

I never saw Ma Thomas again.

Yet, even now, I can still remember the call of seagulls in the night and the sound of surf on the South African coast. Her serene brown eyes still smile at me some nights, and if I stretch out my hand, my index finger searches for that tantalising little dimple in her left buttock. I'm damned if I can recall her face though, or even her first name. Ma Thomas she must remain, the bastard child of a Hottentot harlot and an anonymous British soldier who probably did not even know he was a father.

I JOIN THE POLICE

*S*outhern Africa must surely be one of the most beautiful places on earth. The air is as crisp and invigorating as Arizona, with clear, bright horizons and fruitful soil. It is a place a man can be proud to call home.

The population was more diverse than I expected, with Jewish traders, Hottentots, sunburned British settlers, shaggy-haired Boers in broad hats and the ubiquitous local tribesmen. Whereas in the States I stood out, here I was anonymous, just one black face among thousands.

Having served as an infantryman and as a cavalry trooper, I much preferred the latter. I had no intention of footslogging across Africa when I could ride in relative comfort. Having made that decision, the first thing I needed was a horse.

By that time, I had picked up the basics of the various languages, so I could communicate adequately with most of the people I met. After two days walking, I saw a white man riding a shaggy pony, with another on a long rein behind him. I knew by his clothes and demeanour that he was a Boer, rather than a British settler. He wore brown clothing, was long-haired and long-bearded, with a deeply sun-browned face and a round brown hat. He looked more like an American frontiersman than anything else, so for a moment, I felt a twinge of nostalgia for the old Texas frontier.

"Do you know that man?" I asked a passing Hottentot.

"No," the Tottie shied away. "He's a Boer."

"I know that," I said.

The Boer was of the earth; round-shouldered, riding well back on his horse, with a rifle in a bucket beside his saddle. His horses were unkempt but healthy, both in peak condition. I followed at a distance, far enough back not to be seen, yet sufficiently close not to lose sight of my quarry.

I had all the patience of the Texas frontier and the remainder of my life before me. I followed that Boer horseman for three days ever deeper into Africa, never losing sight of him by day and lying in the bush by night as he slept beside his campfire. On the third night, I removed his rifle and bandolier, slung them across my shoulder and led away his horses. I did not harm the man and smiled to think of his feelings in the morning when he woke to find that I had robbed him.

I had seen some military traffic on the roads. There was infantry, looking remarkably like Johnny Reb or Union soldiers except for the scarlet uniforms, and small units of horsemen, trotting or walking in loose formations. I saw no black faces among the soldiers, which was a disappointment, although many of the wagon drivers were black.

When I heard a shout ahead and saw a horse galloping towards me with its reins flapping loose and a broken girth strap, I knew that God, or William, had sent me a sign.

"Hey!" A man chased the horses, waving his hands and shouting. "Come back! Stop that horse, somebody!"

Waiting until the runaway horse was alongside, I pulled my mount closer to it, leaned over and grabbed the reins.

"Whoa, boy!" I said, pulling gently until the loose horse slowed to a canter. I rode beside it for a few moments, allowing it time to calm down, then spoke quietly until we halted together.

"Well done that, man!" the man spoke English with a cheerful, cultivated accent and wore a blue uniform I had never seen before. His forage cap clung precariously to the back of his head. I thought he was a sailor on land. "Good horsemanship, fellow!"

"Thank you," I said.

The blue-uniformed man scratched his head. "Only the truth, old fellow." He looked at me, openly smiling. "You speak English, you manage a horse like a Sikh cavalryman, and you are helpful and polite; what the devil are you? You're not a Basuto, I can see, and you're no more a Xhosa than I am."

"I'm not a Basuto," I agreed.

"We've agreed upon that," my uniformed man said. He eyed me up and down. "You sound American. You're not from Liberia, are you?"

I was searching for a reply when the uniformed man continued. "I say, you're not looking for a position, are you?"

"I might be," I said. "What is the position?"

"You are? Jolly good! I'm Weston! Lieutenant Weston of the Frontier Armed and Mounted Police. Come along then. What should I call you?"

"Sharpe," I said. "William Sharpe."

So that was how I became a scout for the Frontier Police. It was a step down from a corporal in the 9th US Cavalry to what was an irregular auxiliary, but it suited me at the time.

"I've got a prize here," Lieutenant Weston introduced me. "This fellow is a Liberian, rides like a Cossack and knows English like an Oxford Don!"

The police greeted me with grunts and nods. At first, I was not impressed by the Frontier Police. They seemed lax in their duties, with the officers careless of discipline and the constables merely careless. The day-to-day work was not dissimilar to the 9th Cavalry, if somewhat too casual to my eyes.

The Apaches would mop you boys up, I thought. However, I

listened to all I could, observed their drill and weapons and learned how the British operated.

All the Frontier Police were white, with the guides and scouts black, either Hottentot or Basuto, with a few Fingoes scattered among them. I had hoped to find something better in Africa, although some of the Basutos were farmers, living in a European style, the same as the Boer or British settlers. I had yearned for somewhere I could belong, a civilised black kingdom. I had not found it yet.

Lieutenant Weston was an Englishman, rather than a settler. He was friendly and cheerful, and far tougher than he appeared. I thought he would have done well along the Rio Grande.

The police were based near a small place called Komgha, a village 40 miles or so northeast of King William Town. There was nothing much there except dust, snakes and flies, and the native Africans who came to stare at us as we worked. We started at six in the morning, had various parades and inspections, and the occasional patrol through tranquil countryside. I began to think that Ma Thomas had been wrong with her warnings of an impending war. After experiencing hostile Comanches, Kickapoos and Apaches, I found South Africa to be easy soldiering.

At first.

Further north, the Xhosa, or Kaffirs as they were also known, were giving trouble. The situation was similar to Texas, except with far greater numbers. The overall position was simple: the Boers had been expanding north from the Cape of Good Hope at the same time as the black Africans had been moving south from somewhere in the interior. Sometime in the late 18th century, the vanguard of the Boers met the most advanced tribe of black Africans at the Great Fish River.

Both sides were shocked, for neither expected to see the other. The Boers thought the Lord had granted all of Africa to them, while the Xhosa, the most forward of the black, or bantu, tribes, had never seen a white man. Until then, both black and white had only ever encountered the Bushmen, a very primitive people who had been the original African people. Both the whites and blacks treated the Bushmen like vermin, exterminating or hunting them down for sport. The Boers had also encountered the Hottentots, who were neither white nor black.

From the time of their meeting at the Great Fish River, blacks and Boers, and later the British, had a series of land wars. Both sides wanted land for cattle, and neither would back down.

Even at Komgha, the Frontier Police began to mount more patrols to catch cattle thieves. Closer to Kaffraria, the thieving, raiding and general unrest were more prevalent. As I have indicated elsewhere, the Xhosa were split into several tribes, some more aggressive than others. One of the most hostile was the Galekas, a fine, tall, active and muscular people. Some of the Galekas were acting as servants with the Frontier Police and openly admitted they would return to their country and fight against the British.

"Would you kill the men you work with?" I asked.

"Yes," they said, openly.

"Would you kill me?"

"Yes; you are a servant of the British."

When the border raiding intensified, the Galeka attached the frontier farms. At first, they only stole the livestock, and then they began to kill, plunder and destroy. A senior officer named Maclean called us together, told us the situation and told us we were marching to the frontier.

"Here we go, boys!" Lieutenant Weston said, with a cheroot between his teeth and a smile in his eyes. "Come along, Liberia," he said to me, "we'll need your skills."

We marched from Komgha to the Kei River, the Grand Kei, still relaxed, with the troopers in any formation. The closer we got to the Kei, the more hostile the countryside became, with bands of armed Xhosa watching us, then scurrying away.

"Shall I scout ahead, sir?" I asked Lieutenant Weston.

"Oh, you do that, Liberia," he said. "Don't get yourself killed."

"I'll try not to, sir," I said and trotted ahead of the column. I was relieved to be alone, for to my eyes, such a straggling, amateurish bunch as the Frontier Police were vulnerable to ambush.

On our side of the Kei River was British Kaffraria, while on the opposite side were the free African nations, the people I had dreamed of joining. The major tribes were the Galekas, Pondos, Tambokies, Bomvanas, and Pondamise. Now that I saw them, I wondered what I should do. These Africans seemed more like Apaches than like me, despite our shared skin colour. The most civilised were the Fingoes, who sided with the British. I will write more of the Fingoes later.

Except for the Fingoes, the tribes were superstitious, cruel, and as near to barbarity as I had ever seen. They wore a blanket for clothing, and seemed to hate the white men, fought each other as much as the British and seldom kept their word. Once again, I felt torn between two cultures.

Of them all, the Galekas were the most formidable in battle and the most resolute in opposing the British. The Pondamise were less in numbers and fought on horseback, raiding quickly and returning to their fastnesses. All the tribes had some firearms, but their favoured weapon was the assegai or spear. These came in various types, from the throwing spear to the shorter stabbing variety. If anybody were sufficiently unfortunate to survive an assegai wound, the tribes would kill him by ripping open the belly and stomach. They do that to everybody, living or dead, man, woman or child. Any prisoners would face hideous torture.

The British tried to keep the peace with and between the Xhosa tribes, but that was an impossible task. With a large population of warriors, all hungry for land and cattle – their wealth – and a finite area in which to operate, wars and rumours of wars were endemic. Treaties were made and broken, and made again. Although I had no love for the British for colonising the lands of black people, I could appreciate the courage of the men and women who tried to establish farms on the frontier.

I was experienced in riding through hostile territory, and the terrain of Southern Africa is no more difficult than that of the Southwest United States. I scouted for the Frontier Police, searching for ambushes as we rode among the hills beside the Kei River. The road was terrible, slowing down our wagons, but I'd ridden much worse. We stopped for the night at a place called Toleni. It was here that I discovered the curious police method of tying the horses in a circle under an armed guard. I did not include my horses with the herd. If the Xhosa chose that night to attack, I wanted to be able to mount and ride within a minute. I had no plan to fight to the death with the Frontier Police, for although Weston was a cheerful, friendly man, I felt no loyalty to him or the unit. They were a means to an end, and nothing more.

We were riding through Fingoe land, so in theory, we should have been safe. Yet I was taking no chances. Bullets win battles, not theories. As in America, the native tribes fight each other, which meant the Galekas were as likely to raid the Fingoes as they were to attack the British settlers. At one time, the Fingoes were a minor tribe, which left them open to attack by their neighbours. The Galekas used them as slaves, which shocked me. I was unhappy to find black people having other blacks as slaves. When the British arrived, they freed the Fingoes from slavery, and since then the Fingoes have prospered as allies of the British. Of all the tribes on this frontier, the Fingoes seemed the most civilised. As I rode on my scouting expeditions, I considered finding a plump Fingoe woman and settling down here.

We camped beside the Kei, the police still casual, although the artillery pieces they dragged were a reminder of the realities of war. As the police sat around the camp-fires, singing and smoking, the scouts rode around to gather information. After a day or so, the officers drilled the police, making them ready for the war everybody knew was coming.

I found a local woman, enjoyed her bright smile and allowed her to perfect my knowledge of the local languages and other cultures. She – I can't remember her name – she told me that the Galeka chiefs had called together their witch doctors to foresee the future. That was ominous to my ears, for the Kiowas and Comanche always held religious services before the young braves took the warpath. When the Frontier Police had a church service the next Sunday, and the hymns rang out over the African bush, I wondered if they were not also seeking divine help in the next war. Cultures have more similarities than differences, I think. I took part in a few patrols, learning the topography, and then, late in October 1877, the troubles escalated along the frontier.

"Liberia!" Lieutenant Weston gestured to me.

I hurried across to him. "Sir!"

"You've been learning the country. Now's your chance to show us how good you are. Find out what that firing is all about."

I told the lieutenant that I had not heard any firing.

"I have," he said at once. "Artillery and musketry. Off you go, Liberia, and watch your back."

Perhaps the wind shifted, or Lieutenant Weston's ears were sharper than mine, for shortly after, I heard the firing, like distant thunder, punctured by the sharper crackle of rifles. I mounted up and rode towards the sound.

I GO TO WAR AGAIN

I heard later that the Galekas had attacked the Fingoe
reservation, and the British sent a detachment of
Frontier Police with a 7-pounder cannon to help their allies. As I
rode towards the firing, a scattering of Fingoes ran past me,
fleeing in the opposite direction. It was only with difficulty that I
stopped a couple to ask what was happening.

"They're all dead," one stalwart man said, with his eyes
staring.

"Who's all dead?" I asked.

"The white police," he said. "The Galekas massacred them
all." He ran off, leaving me wondering.

The next man told me the same story, so I checked my rifle
was loaded and balanced it across my knee as I moved on.

As more Fingoes appeared, all with the same story, I put
spurs to my horse and hurried towards the fighting. The firing
escalated and then stopped. I heard, drifting on the wind, a
rising chorus of singing, and Southern African tribes can sing
like no other. It sounded like a victory chant, which I saw a
disciplined force of blue-coated men coming towards me, towing
a single cannon.

"Sir!" I saluted the inspector in charge. "Lieutenant Weston asked me to find out what was happening." I knew by their demeanour and powder-blackened faces that these men had recently been in action.

The officer was Inspector Chalmers, who ignored me. One of the NCOs told me that the police had engaged the Galekas, who had driven them back with the loss of six men. I wished to see for myself, so I rode to a small rise overlooking the battlefield, which was near a hill called Guadana.

Until that day, I had no idea of the numbers involved in these encounters with the tribes of South Africa. I had imagined the actions to be like our wars with the Indians, with raiding bands of a few dozen, or a few hundred at most. When I saw the Galeka army celebrating, I was astonished at the numbers; there must have been 4000 warriors there. I withdrew in haste to report to Lieutenant Weston, who listened to my report with a solemn expression on his face.

"Thousands of them, eh?" He produced two cheroots, lit one, and handed the other to me. "I've seen you with a pipe," he said. "Try one of these."

"Thank you, sir," I said.

"Now go and get ready," the lieutenant said. "If the Galekas choose to attack, things could get sticky here." He gave his usual bright smile. "That's why we're here, though, isn't it? We protect the weak from the aggressors for the sake of Good Queen Vic? That's what the British Empire is all about."

"Yes, sir," I said.

I would estimate the police at under 200 strong, with perhaps 1500 unreliable Fingoe allies, while I later heard that the Galekas had 5000 warriors, many with firearms, all with assegais.

The police withdrew to camp and prepared to defend themselves against a Galeka attack which, fortunately, never happened. Lieutenant Weston toured his men, giving advice, checking their rifles, cracking jokes and smoking his cheroot. Even with the Galekas poised only a few miles away, the atmosphere in the camp was light-hearted. They joked about dying and made bets who would survive.

I held William's pipe, looked over my shoulder and wondered if I should remain with the police or leave. I owed them no loyalty.

"Still with us, Liberia?" Lieutenant Weston grinned to me. "Good man!" He walked on, laughing, as many of our Fingoe allies drifted away.

The Galekas did not attack. If they had, they could have swept us away, although one is never sure with the British. I remained with the police. A few days later, Chalmers sent me with a patrol to locate the bodies of the six police. When we found them, I knew that the Apaches could not teach the Galekas anything about mutilation. Each policeman had been stripped naked, and the Galekas had ripped open their stomachs. The Galekas had scalped one policeman and had butchered the others in various ways. Until that discovery, the police had been a good-natured unit, but now they altered. They growled like fighting dogs.

I had heard that the British were the most civilised of the European powers, known for their good manners, tolerance and humanity. They were the first empire in the world to end slavery, and the British flag was a beacon of freedom. All that may well have been true, but when they saw their companions mutilated, I swear that the British became as savage as the worst of humanity. Some even glared at me, as if I were responsible for the horrors.

After the Battle of Guadana, as we called the skirmish, and finding the bodies, there was less laughter in the police ranks. They had never despised the Galekas as an enemy, but now they sought revenge.

When we realised that the Galekas were not going to launch an immediate attack, we marched to a place called Ibeka, on the very border of Fingoland and Galekaland. Although not perfect, Ibeka was easier to defend than our previous camp. The laughing, capering British became as professional as any soldiers I had ever seen. Ibeka was little more than a trader's store, with stables and outbuildings, and a stone and turf wall surrounding the whole. The police made Ibeka into an armed camp, while I lived under one of the fine blue-gum trees, which provided shade from the fierce African sun.

While I patrolled the local area, the police established a hospital, magazine and officers' quarters. The troopers and such Fingoes as remained with us dug trenches for the riflemen, strengthened the wall and built bastions for our three artillery pieces, all facing the front, from where the Galekas were most likely to attack.

"They only know the frontal attack and simple ambushes," Weston said and grinned. "I hope!"

At night, we patrolled the area, with standing and mobile pickets, with horsemen crossing and re-crossing the surrounding area.

I took my full part in all this, riding by day, and picketing by night, although I noticed most NCOs ensured a white trooper accompanied me. They did not fully trust a black foreigner – although, being British, I do not think they fully trusted any foreigner, whatever his colour.

The men slept fully clothed, with their rifles to hand in case of an attack. They carried the Snider rifle, a single-shot breech-loader, developed by Jacob Snider of New York. At first, I was a little contemptuous, thinking these rifles inferior to the Spencers and Springfields we had used in Texas, but the Sniders were also accurate, with less chance of accidental discharge. The British could fire ten aimed rounds a minute, with ranges up to a thousand yards, and twice that many un-aimed. I had heard that the British soldiers were poor shots and liked to stand in long lines of red coats to provide targets for their enemies. These Frontier Police were as good shots as our frontiersmen and as adept at finding cover.

I happened to be on patrol when the Galekas approached,

and I galloped back to Ibeka with my police trooper at my side. The Galekas were about 500 strong, well-mounted and armed with a variety of firearms as well as assegais. This frontier must have a version of Comancheros, I thought.

"They're carrying a white flag," my companion, a man named Buchan, said. "Maybe they want to surrender to us." He grinned across to me.

We watched when a small group detached from the main body and rode boldly towards Ibeka, with the flag hanging limp in the sun.

"That's Sidgow, one of Chief Kreli's sons," Buchan said. Buchan was a red-haired, freckled Scotsman with a strong accent and skin that peeled with the sun. I heard he had been a soldier and decided to settle in South Africa after his military service.

Using an interpreter, Sidgow told us that he was very sorry that his people had killed the policemen, for the Galekas only wanted peace with the white men. He said that the Fingoes had been stealing Galeka cattle, which was why the Galeka had attacked them. Captain Robinson of the police rode out to talk to Sidgow and called me over as an interpreter, for he did not trust the Galeka's man.

As the two leaders spoke, 500 Galeka horsemen waited in shifting ranks, observing our defences. In turn, the police stood behind the wall and in the trenches, Sniders ready and fingers hovering on the triggers.

Sidgow said he intended to attack the Fingoes, and asked Captain Robinson to stand aside and allow him access to Fingoeland.

"In other words," Robinson said, "we have to let these vagabonds loot, maim, burn, rape and murder."

In all my experience of warrior tribes, I had never heard anything so strange. Captain Robinson, in charge of a small garrison, refused to take his men out of danger. His duty was to protect the Fingoes, so that is what he would do. Robinson pointed to the cannon, told Sidgow that each piece was loaded with case shot, and ordered the Galekas to return to their country and leave the Fingoes in peace.

After a few moments, Sidgow and his men withdrew. Only the tension remained.

"They'll be back," Weston said, puffing at a cheroot, "and they'll bring their friends with them."

Nobody in Ibeka supposed that the affair would end there. Captain Robinson sent out patrols to scout the area, and we found that the Galekas had gathered around 3000 men only a few miles away. I saw this force, thousands of armed black Africans, and wondered if I were on the wrong side. I had wanted to join a powerful African king, and Kreli of the Galekas undoubtedly had a large army. Yet, I knew that the Galekas were nothing compared to the Zulus further north. I decided to stay where I was for a space and see what happened.

Robinson sent out more patrols, with orders to observe, gather information and report back. I rode out more than once, each time seeing large bodies of Galekas marching towards Kreli's kraal – his palace and village – which was only eight miles or so from Ibeka.

Occasionally, our patrols exchanged shots with the Galekas, with no casualties on our side, and probably none on theirs. Robinson sent messages to the authorities in Cape Town, telling them of the seriousness of the situation, without reply. It was quarter of a century since the last Xhosa – or Kaffir – War and the government refused to believe there would be another.

While the government buried its head in the sand, we continued to patrol and gather what reinforcements we could from the Fingoes.

To the east of our camp, a slope rose to a stone-scattered ridge, on the opposite side of which ran the Xoxa River. The land was level to the north and west and peppered with boulders that would give cover to an attacking force. To our front, the ground descended for a mile, with hollows in which an attacker could shelter. It was not an ideal situation, but better than any other in the immediate locality. We had the advantage of disciplined firepower and three cannon, but the artillery could only cover the south side, the front, of Ibeka.

Our camp sat right on the frontier of Fingoeland and Galekaland. About a hundred yards in front of our defensive perimeter, a small pile of stones marked the border.

The patrols continued. A new commander arrived, Commandant Griffiths, and took command of Ibeka without show or fuss. He reduced our garrison by sending men away to outlying posts. We watched the troopers ride out, counted our ammunition and waited.

We sat in the camp with 120 Frontier Police, a handful of European colonists and about 2000 Fingoes, commanded by another Scotsman, named Allan Maclean. I felt the atmosphere tighten. I could taste the tension in the air and knew that something was going to happen.

As so often, I was out on patrol along with Buchan. We came across a couple of Galeka woman gathering sticks, and I asked them if there was any news. They told me that Kreli was coming to attack Ibeka.

"We've been hearing that for weeks," I said. "When is this miracle going to happen?"

"Soon," they said and walked away with immense dignity.

Buchan led the way around a rocky bluff, then reined up. "Look," he said.

About a mile ahead, I saw a dense mass of black humanity. That was the first time I had seen an African army, and it was far more impressive than I had expected.

The Galekas were about 8000 strong, a much larger army than the Indians had ever mustered against us in Texas, or anywhere else in the States, I believe. Although I was fighting with the British, I felt a pang of brotherhood to see so many black African warriors.

"Come on, Liberia," Buchan said. "It's not healthy here."

We returned to Ibeka with the news, and about eight in the morning, our outlying pickets fell back.

"They're coming!" the pickets reported, more calmly than I would have expected.

We stood to our arms, aware that defeat meant death, either by bullet or assegai, for the Galeka did not take prisoners. We stood at positions behind the walls and in the rifle trenches, with the gunners lounging over their barrels.

"You're still with us, Liberia?" Lieutenant Weston arrived at my side, cheroot in mouth and his forage cap pushed to the back of his head. "Good man." He walked away, hands in pockets, to check on his men.

The Galeka army halted a little over a mile away, in near perfect silence, thousands of African warriors in a display of force I had never thought to see. Sunlight played on them, reflecting on the blades of assegais and the locks and barrels of rifles.

"Why are they waiting?" a young policeman asked.

"So we get scared," Buchan told him.

The police did not look scared. They glowered towards the Galekas, patting the stocks of their rifles, smoking and making grim jokes, as is the British way. As the Galekas stood, we readied ourselves for the coming battle. After a hurried breakfast, we saddled the horses, opened ammunition boxes and spaced them around the firing positions. "Water," Weston said and ensured there were kegs of fresh water ready. "Fighting is thirsty work."

I agreed with him.

"You've seen some fighting, then?" He was sharp, that man.

"Some, sir," I replied.

"Not in Liberia, I think," Weston said. "You're not from Liberia, are you?" He ran his gaze down my body.

"No, sir."

"I didn't think so. What were you? Come on, out with it! It'll go no further."

"9th US Cavalry," I said, feeling my back straighten as I spoke.

"Damned good!" Weston said. "Good to have you with us, Buffalo Soldier." He held out his hand. That was the first time an officer had made that gesture. It was also the first time I had seen the British prepare for battle. They were very professional, yet laughed and joked with a nonchalance I had not expected. Some were whistling, others smoking their pipes and laying outside the tents, waiting for the call to action. Most waited behind the wall, or in the rifle trenches. Buchan was fast asleep in the shadow of the wall, with his forage cap over his face.

Further back, perhaps a mile into their territory, the Fingoes were also waiting, with Allan Maclean walking among them, a lone white man amidst hundreds of black warriors.

"Listen, boys," Weston called out, his voice unnaturally loud in the tense hush. "One of our spies has reported that the Gaikas might join the Galekas. If the Galekas overrun us, the whole frontier will be ablaze; it will be another major Xhosa War, and with the Zulus or even the Boers restless, we might lose the colonies. Fight well, boys."

As the police digested this new information, Weston winked at me. "Do you need some exercise, Buffalo Soldier?"

A minute later we were riding out towards the Galeka's position, with Weston a length ahead of me, cheroot in mouth and his forage cap rammed on the back of his head. "Come on, Buffalo Soldier!" He spurred his horse, bringing us within half a mile of the Galeka army. "Can you see that?"

Hundreds of Galeka horsemen were reinforcing their army. "I count 2000," I said.

"So do I," Weston said, "and some are heading this way."

We returned at speed, with a dozen Galeka riders galloping behind us. They reined up when a section of police fired a volley.

"Get ready, lads!" Weston shouted as we jumped our horses over the wall and reined up within the perimeter of the camp.

"There's about 2000 cavalry on the ridge to our left, and columns of infantry to the front."

I had expected an immediate massed frontal attack, but the Galekas were more disciplined. They ordered skirmishers to the front, riflemen who fired the minute they came within range. As bullets whined over our heads, the British responded by sending out hundreds of Fingoes, while a skirmish line of police supported our allied tribesmen.

"On you come, Buffalo," Weston shouted. "You too, Buchan!" We pushed our horses over the wall once more, with the mass of Galekas advancing towards us, their columns wreathed in gun smoke.

I saw the mounted Galeka crest the ridge. Our artillery fired, but the first shells were too high and did no damage. The Galeka infantry pushed on, approaching the camp in their thousands. We fired rockets next, which proved much more effective. I saw great rifts appear in the Galeka mounted ranks, with many of their horses, and some of the men, running in panic.

"Fire at them, Buffalo!" Weston shouted, and I obeyed, firing my rifle into the mass of advancing Galekas, reloading and firing again. The Fingoes roared into the Galeka skirmishers, hacking and stabbing with the deadly assegais.

A British bugle sounded retire, and Weston called us back, clearing the way for the three 7-pounders to open fire on the infantry.

"This could be interesting," Weston said as the first artillery shells landed amid the Galeka columns. "I doubt they've experienced artillery before."

Even from this distance, I could sense the Galeka surprise as their casualties mounted. They kept coming, firing with their rifles, brandishing their assegais, yelling their warcries. When the artillery smashed their columns, I thought they would retire, but instead, they formed skirmish lines and attacked in open clouds. We drove them back and they reformed, to come again and again, horse and foot together. I was proud of these men, even as I killed them. We stopped their charges about fifty yards from the defensive wall, although a few came closer and threw their assegais. Dead Galeka bodies formed a high-tide mark to show the extent of their advances.

I was impressed by the tenacity of the attack and the staunchness of the defence. The Galekas fought with bravery, and the British with skill as the fight continued all day, only ending after a final massed charge at five in the afternoon. The Galekas rushed, all the survivors together, undaunted by their earlier losses as they advanced over the shattered bodies of their colleagues. The British met them with Sniders, shells and rockets, some policemen standing up to aim better. I saw Buchan mount the wall, loading and firing like a man possessed, his face a mask of concentration. Lieutenant Weston walked up and down his section of the wall, exposing himself to enemy fire as he encouraged, exhorted and fired at the Galekas. He occasionally stopped to help a man clear a jammed rifle, or hand out ammunition.

When the Galekas made their final attack, our bullets stopped them. They wavered, with a great shiver running through their ranks.

"They're beat, boys," Lieutenant Weston said. "They know they can't take Ibeka."

"Come on, my lads!" Allan Maclean shouted, charging forward into the Galekas' flank. "Come on, my bonny Fingoes!" He led from the front with hundreds of Fingoes behind him, thrusting and stabbing with their assegais. On the opposite flank, Inspector John Maclean did the same with 50 mounted police.

Unable to penetrate our fire and attacked on both flanks, the Galekas broke and fled, with our artillery pursuing them until they were out of range. I reloaded and looked around to count our casualties. Forty Fingoes had died, and not a single policeman. For all the fire and fury, the Galeka musketry had been ineffective.

"They always fire too high," Buchan said, casually. "You fought well, Buffalo."

"So did you," I said.

He nodded to me, which was probably a big a compliment as I ever got in my life.

I could not count the Galeka casualties. They were in the hundreds, men killed by rifle bullets or assegais, some torn to pieces with shellfire. The Fingoes were busy dispatching the wounded, as seemed to be the way in African warfare.

As always after a battle, there was no elation, only exhaustion and depression. Heavy rain added to the misery. We remained at our posts in case the Galekas returned to the attack, taking it in turns to sleep as the sounds of the African night seemed more oppressive than usual.

"They might sneak up on us in the dark," a young policeman said.

"Keep alert, then," Buchan said.

We kept alert, dripping rainwater from sodden forage caps, pointing our rifle barrels downwards and protecting the locks with rags and old socks to keep them dry.

"It's in weather like this that assegais are better weapons," the same young policeman said.

"You swap your Snider for a spear if you wish," Buchan suggested, sourly.

Towards dawn, after a miserable, uneventful night, Lieutenant Weston touched my shoulder.

"Come on, Buffalo," the lieutenant seemed tireless. "Let's see what's happening out there."

We had hardly left the camp when the rain stopped. There was no gradual easing; one moment we huddled before the torrent, and the next, there was no rain. Simultaneously, as if by heavenly decree, the sun emerged.

"Well now," Weston said, pulling up his horse. "That was fortunate."

I agreed. If we had continued in the dark, we would have

ridden straight into the entire Galeka army, which had returned to the position it occupied before the battle.

"Back we go, Buffalo," Weston said. "There are more men on the ridge. Brave fellows, these Galekas."

The instant we returned to camp, our artillery opened fire, landing shells on the enemy positions over 2000 yards distant. The Galekas came on, yet without the same fervour as the previous day. At 1000 yards, extreme range, we opened up with the rifles, firing volleys to augment the artillery. The Galekas came twice more, each time advancing a lesser distance, and then they retired.

"That's the last we'll see of them for a while," Lieutenant Weston said with satisfaction. He handed back the rifle he had borrowed. "Come on again, Buffalo. You too, Buchan. We'll see if they're lurking anywhere."

They were not. The Galeka army had vanished as if they had never been, leaving only their dead and the human detriment that all troops create.

I AM STILL AT WAR

*T*hat battle marked the beginning of a war that people seem to have forgotten, unlike the later British-Zulu War. In my experience, both had equal heroism, although the British awarded many more medals for fighting the Zulus. The Xhosa War was my introduction to Africa, and in it, I saw both the strengths and weaknesses of the African tribes.

With the Galeka assault repulsed, the government in Cape Town decided to reinforce the frontier.

"Here come the redcoats," Buchan said, as a British regular regiment, the 24th Foot, marched in, all scarlet coats, sun helmets, blue trousers and Martini-Henry rifles. Augmenting them were a mixture of British settlers and great-bearded Boer burghers. At the back, chattering as they sharpened their assegais, hundreds of Fingoes joined the army, eager to destroy their one-time slave masters.

Within a couple of days of the battle, the Fingoes captured Kreli's witch doctor, a woman called Nita. The Galeka claimed that Nita had led their attack on Ibeka, or at least had persuaded them to try. She had encouraged the Galekas by giving the warriors charms of hair and wood which, she claimed, would make them invulnerable to British bullets.

The Fingoes were as superstitious as the Galekas, so ended the witch's power by a quick decapitation, bringing both head and body into our camp in triumph. We all crowded around to see the infamous Nita. Her body was covered with tattoos, plus she had rings and chains attached to her limbs. Nita was the first witch doctor I had seen, and I can say that, although dead, she had a powerful face. I can see it now, glaring up at me through wide-open eyes. The Fingoes mocked her, and it was one of our policeman, a Scottish Highlander, who crossed himself when he saw the head.

"She's still watching us," he said. "It's better not to meddle with heathen gods."

Those words remain with me yet.

I can also see the face of Gangeleswe, chief of the Tamboukies. He was the very opposite of Nita, a man of the lowest type, whatever his skin colour and race. Gangeleswe liked to beat his wives to a pulp, lie, cheat and deceive his own people. Nobody trusted his promises, but the British allowed him onto their lands, where I would have put a bullet in his black heart, or hanged him from the nearest tree.

Other chiefs came into Ibeka to profess the undying friendship they had forgotten until the late British-Fingoe victory. One, in particular, Mapassa, a Galeka chief, the British allowed to cross into, and settle in, British territory. Mapassa, with his followers and women, aided first the Galekas and later the Gaikas against the British. Again, the British were too soft. They should have hanged the man and sent his followers back into Galekaland.

That is my opinion as a soldier.

While the British harboured every runaway and spy who came begging, they also prepared to invade Galekaland. Meanwhile, Kreli was gathering his forces and recruiting warriors from all the neighbouring tribes.

About two weeks after the Battle of Ibeka, the British and I invaded Galekaland, with Kreli's Kraal our objective. We moved in three columns about 12 miles apart. The column I was in had two cannon and two days rations, for Kreli's Kraal was not far from the frontier. After a false start, we left Ibeka about two in the morning, following a reasonable track that led straight to the kraal.

I was one of the scouts, with Buchan beside me. We were wary, expecting the Galeka to attack, something they failed to do. We reached Kreli's Kraal without firing a single shot, and I was not impressed. I had hoped for something better than a large hut, which Kreli's palace was, surrounded by several other huts, all within a simple stockade.

The Galeka warriors were camped around, without a single sentry or outpost, in a very slovenly manner. We surrounded the place, volunteer settlers, Frontier Police and Fingoes, waited for the sound of a bugle, and attacked. I think we achieved total surprise, for the defenders only fired a few shots and fled in a gap between the Fingoes and the settlers.

As seems typical in this type of campaign, bloody battles and hard marches feature between periods of boredom, introspection and confusion. In our case, we also had frustration. From Kreli's Kraal, a group of Fingoes guided us to Lusisi, about 35 miles away through rounded, beautiful hills. I did not know why we were there. I only know that the troops were grumbling, the rations were late, if they came at all, and always inadequate. We camped in a hollow through which a river ran, and with bush and trees along the sides. To the front, the land was open for perhaps a mile.

"Who chose this place?" Buchan asked. "It's an invitation to be ambushed."

"The officers know what they're doing, Jock," another policeman said. All the English troopers called the Scotsmen "Jock". It was a derogatory, racial term, like "Kaffir" for the blacks. Britain was not a single nation, I learned, but a combination of four, England, Wales, Scotland and Ireland, with the English assuming a superiority that men from the other three countries found amusing and irritating in equal measure.

"Are you sure the officers know what they're doing?" Buchan said. "I'll keep my rifle by my side. "You lads should do the same."

I agreed with Buchan. We exchanged knowing glances, two veterans with a single mind.

It rained that night, raising the river level and increasing our misery. Buchan and I were on picket duty, sheltering under a tree and staring into the dark, listening for sounds through the constant hammer of the rain.

I sensed something, although I did not know what, and alerted Buchan with a low whistle.

"Aye," Buchan said, quietly. "I feel it."

We moved forward a few steps, rifles at the ready, stopping when thunder growled above us. A sudden flash of lightning blinded us both.

"Galekas," Buchan said. "Waiting ahead."

I had seen them too; hundreds of warriors crouching down, ignoring the rain. We withdrew quietly to warn the others.

The Galekas came with the dawn, 500 strong as they rushed the camp. We were ready for them, meeting their attack with volley fire, so a general engagement began. That was the most confusing battle I was ever in, what with the heavy rain and the thick forest, both sides firing, smoke from the rifles, and men appearing and disappearing between the trees. When we sent the Fingoes to hunt the Galekas, it was almost impossible to tell friend from foe. We had to be very careful who we shot.

A couple of hours after the battle began, the Galekas suddenly broke and fled. We pursued them until the thick bush and mist made it impossible to see more than a few yards in front of us.

"I think that's far enough, boys," Lieutenant Weston said. "We'll lose ourselves in this muck, and the Galekas will surely be long gone by now."

We returned through wet bush to the equally wet camp to hear that the Fingoes had found a band of Galekas hidden in a cave.

I did not take part in the expedition to flush them out, although I heard the details later. A couple of Border farmers, the Goss brothers, led a force of Fingoes to remove the Galekas. They found the Galekas in a long cave with a narrow entrance some five feet above the ground, advanced, and were driven back by accurate rifle fire. The Goss brothers led a frontal assault, where the Galekas killed them both, and only Fingoe subtlety won the day. The Fingoes lured a Galeka outside and killed him with an assegai. Then they rushed inside the cave, massacring all the warriors.

Once again, the British had won the battle, and the usual depression set in afterwards. The heavy rain continued, soaking us all, and the starvation rations made things worse. The Fingoes had to help the police, supplying us with their mealies, as the Africans call maize. The next few days were the most miserable I spent since Cape Horn, with incessant rain, little food and no rest.

I had heard the mutterings of discontent, so was not surprised when the police rebelled when the officers ordered us to move.

"No," came the reply. "We're not moving until the officers feed us."

Lieutenant Weston wandered over, damp cheroot in mouth and a whimsical smile on his face. "What's this all about, lads?"

The constables announced their grievances, exaggerating their hunger, as people always exaggerate when they think themselves hard done by. The lieutenant listened, nodded, and returned to the commandant.

Within a day, a waggon load of provisions appeared. We all ate until we could eat no more, with Buchan and one other of the constables even giving some of their rations to the Fingoes.

When the commandant threatened the ringleaders with punishment, the men laughed.

"They broke the contract," Buchan said.

We marched the next morning, one of three columns intended to scour Galekaland for the enemy. The plan was to drive them towards a military post called Fort Bowker, 25 miles east of Guadana Hill. The post had a sizeable garrison who would meet the Galekas head-on, and between us, we could destroy their army.

However, I was not destined to see the end of that operation. My time as a Police Scout ended abruptly.

I was riding out, with Buchan at my side, happy to be fed and mobile again, when I heard the shout in a heavy Boer accent.

"Hey! You! The black scout!"

Buchan glanced at me. "He means you, Buffalo."

I looked over my shoulder, wondering if I was being sent on another scouting mission, or if I had been guilty of some infraction of the rules. I started when I recognised the Boer who advanced on me with his hand outstretched.

"Those are my horses! That's my rifle! That Kaffir is a thief!"

I might have been able to convince the Frontier Police of my innocence, but the Boers always thought the worst of the Africans. I kicked in my spurs and sped away as fast as I could. I immediately knew that my time as a police scout had ended as suddenly as it had begun.

"Stop that Kaffir!" the Boer said, racing after me.

My route took me over the shoulder of a hill, and when I reached the crest, I looked behind me to see Buchan, that most loyal of men, had blocked the Boer's path with his horse and was arguing with him, preventing him from following me.

"Thank you, Buchan," I said, kicked in my heels and moved away.

I had now left the Frontier Police and was alone in Africa.

I GAIN MY NAME

I rode hard for an hour before stopping to consider my position. What should I do now? I could return to Ma Thomas and resume my easy life there unless somebody else had taken my space in her bed. I could find myself a berth on a ship and try to get back to America, or I could pursue my original dream and find myself a position as a soldier in the army of an African king.

"When we're home in Africa," William's words seemed to mock me as I stood under a rocky ridge, alone, virtually penniless and unsure what to do.

I was already aware there was no choice. I would make my way to the most powerful African king I knew and offer him my services. That king was Cetswayo of the Zulus. That meant I had about 500 miles to ride, over terrain I did not know and which could well contain hostile tribes. I had left my spare horse behind with the police, so I only had the one mount. Well, I had travelled further in the past, and at least in Africa, a black face was not likely to attract suspicion. I resolved to avoid the main roads and cities, hunt what game I could, and move quickly.

Crossing into Fingoeland, I bartered my police uniform for a simple blanket and loincloth, with a pair of European trousers as well. My trading partner was delighted to become an honorary member of the Frontier Police and paraded his treasure to all his friends as I rode away. I aimed to get out of the area as fast as I could, in case the authorities instituted a search for me. I thought that unlikely, with the present war, but with the British, one never knows. They are strange people.

Travelling in the early morning and evening, and resting at night and in the heat of the day, I moved northward. I will not write details of my journey here, partly because I cannot recall them, partly because they will be repetitive. Suffice to say that I travelled alone, crossed high mountains and green plains, forded a hundred rivers and saw animals that I had only ever read about. I passed through the territories of a score of tribes and sub-tribes, finding some friendly and some not. When I mentioned the Zulus, they spoke with fear, loathing or admiration, but always with respect. Every night and every morning, I talked to William as I sat beside my fire, and every time, I sensed his presence.

I moved north, slowly, until I came to another land of white people, where Boer farms and British farms spread out, with substantial square houses, broad roads and fences. It was a prosperous green land, and I knew I was in Natal, not far from the borders of Zululand. Avoiding the cities where white men may still have been looking for me, I eventually came to a broad brown river.

"The Thukela," I said, knowing that this stretch of water marked the border of the most powerful independent kingdom in southern Africa. "When we are home in Africa," I said, fingering William's pipe, "we will laugh at this. Maybe we can be home in the land of the Zulus."

The river was not a significant obstacle. I forded without difficulty, swam my horse through the deeper central section and walked him into Zululand. I knew that, for the first time in my life, I was breathing the free air of Africa.

It did not take long for the Zulus to find me. An hour after I entered the country, a small impi, or regiment of men, appeared. My first indication of their presence was a swirl in the long grass through which I was riding, and then they appeared, a score of men with long shields and stabbing assegais, surrounding me.

I greeted them formally and asked to speak to their chief.

They looked at me for a long moment, with the men lifting their assegais ready to strike. I knew immediately that these men were different from the Galekas or any other warrior I had so far met in Africa. They were fiercer, wilder, and freer; European-style civilization had not tainted them. I was witnessing the real Africa, and I liked what I sensed, although I knew as was as near to death as I had ever been.

"Come," the leader said and moved away at a fast jog. The other men lowered their assegais, formed around me and took me with them, moving easily at the speed of a cantering horse and covering the ground without a word.

They were tall men, not as broad in the chest as I had expected, but lithe and supple, without an ounce of excess fat on them. Within an hour, they arrived at a small village set on a hill, with a barrier of thorns to keep out any prowling animals. Without pause, the warriors escorted me through a neat collection of circular huts to a larger hut in the centre of the village.

"Wait," the leader of my escort said.

I waited while the leader entered the hut. My escort was immobile, facing me with their assegais in their hands, watching everything I did. The leader was perhaps twenty minutes inside the chief's hut before he emerged.

"Go in," he said. "Leave your horse and gun here."

I did so and entered the hut, crawling through the low doorway with my heart beating faster. I had been in a few native huts but never one belonging to a Zulu chief.

The interior was dark and smoky, with a brooding, corpulent man sitting on a small stool. He looked at me for some time before speaking. "Who are you?"

I gave him the name I grew up with, the name that is written on the 9th Cavalry records.

He nodded. "Are you the Buffalo Soldier? The one that stole the Boer's horse?"

That shook me. I had not expected the story of that theft to have reached Zululand, or this chief to work out who I was. "I am," I admitted.

"You will not use your other name here," the chief told me. "If the British or the Boers hear, they will demand we hand you back to be executed."

I nodded. "What shall I call myself?"

"You are Inyathi, the buffalo."

"Inyathi," I repeated the name. "It is a good name."

"Why have you come to the land of the Zulus, Inyathi?" The chief leaned slightly closer to me.

"I want to join the Zulu Army," I said, truthfully. "I have experience as a soldier in America and against the Galekas."

"The Galeka are dogs," the chief said. He passed over a gourd of milk and watched me drink. "You will eat and spend the night at my kraal. Tomorrow you will go to the king at Ulundi."

The decision was made.

Next morning, my escort took me deep into Zululand, trotting by my side without apparent effort. The country was of smooth rolling hills, sweet grass, clear water and patches of forest. Young herd-boys tended herds of cattle, while women walked the paths in more safety than in many American cities.

Since my arrival in Africa, I had heard about the ferocious Zulu warriors and the horrors of Zululand. I saw instead a land at peace with itself, a land of kraals and chiefs, of high skies and the sound of cattle.

The names sounded like angel's music, Umfolozi and Nkandia, Silutshana and Nlobame, Qudeni and Nkandia and the queen of them all, the royal kraal of Ulundi. I savoured the experience of travelling through a black African kingdom, touched William's pipe and repeated our words.

"When we're home in Africa."

On the second morning, we passed a military kraal, where an impi – a regiment – of warriors mustered to inquire our business.

"We're on the King's business," my escort said, and we passed on without incident. That was my first sight of a Zulu impi, each man the same age, with the same array of feathers and furs, the same bundle of assegais and the same black shields.

"Why are their shields black?" I asked the captain of my escort.

"The younger the impi, the darker the shield," the captain told me. "The more veteran the impi, the lighter the shield."

I nodded, impressed by the simplicity of this method of determining the regiments apart.

We reached Ulundi the next day. The royal kraal was vast, much larger than any I had seen, although built to the same basic pattern. The name meant the Heights, the Zulu term for the great Drakensberg, the Dragon Mountains to the west. On my first sight, I knew it was a royal kraal; the sheer scale meant it could be nothing else. My escort approached Ulundi with every sign of respect.

An entire impi was exercising outside the barrier of thorns that surrounded the kraal. When I asked, the captain of my escort told me they were the uVe, 3,500 strong. Cetswayo, the king, had raised them as one of his regiments, with each man now 23 years old, and as I could see by the lack of any isicoco, or head ring, every man was unmarried.

I will write about the Zulu military organisation later. That day my escort brought me inside the royal kraal with its hundreds of huts and constant lowing of cattle. When anybody questioned us, the captain answered he was on the king's business, and nobody hampered our progress. The king's word was law.

The royal hut was in the centre of the kraal, larger than any I had yet seen.

"Wait," the captain of my escort ordered and entered the hut on hands and knees.

I waited outside, as my escort chanted "Bayete" – the royal salute, three times in succession.

I dismounted, calming my suddenly restless horse, and continued to wait. I do not know how long I stood there, but it seemed like hours before the captain returned.

"The king will see you now," he said.

"Ngiyabonga – thank you," I said, taking a deep breath. I could hardly believe what was happening. Here I was, once a slave, a Buffalo Soldier and a lowly seaman, going to meet an African king. I felt the blood rush from my head at the honour and hoped I would not faint or otherwise disgrace myself.

I crawled in the low doorway, and a hard foot kept me in that position as I approached the king.

Cetswayo sat on a carved stool in the centre of the hut. He eyed me in silence for a full five minutes before he spoke, which allowed me the opportunity to observe him. Cetswayo was tall and well-built, if slightly corpulent. He was not flamboyant, as were the European monarchs I had seen in pictures. His bearing was regal, dignified, without the arrogance that I had expected.

When he spoke, his voice was deep, and his words measured. "Why have you come to Zululand?"

"I want to join Your Majesty's army," I said and added. "I want somewhere to belong, Your Majesty; I want to feel like a free man." I lowered my voice, for I had not expected to speak so openly to a king. "I want to be at home."

Cetswayo nodded, his eyes deeply intelligent. "Why in my kingdom?"

I told the king that I had been a slave and a soldier. I told him about the Civil War and my life as a Buffalo Soldier. I told him about life at sea and with the Frontier Police. I was surprised that he listened.

"You have travelled far," Cetswayo said. "You may have a home in my kingdom." He pondered for a moment. "What name shall we call you?"

I told him my name, the name that might still be on the muster rolls of the 9th Cavalry, and I told him the name I had used since then. Then I told him my Zulu name.

"Inyathi," Cetswayo said. "You have no other name in my kingdom."

I have never used any other name since that day.

For the next few days, the king made me prove my skills in front of his indunas and war-captains. These men had fought neighbouring tribes and the Boers; they were seasoned veterans of hand-to-hand combat, men who had thrust their assegais into the bodies of the king's enemies. They would not let any foreign charlatan dupe their king with sugar-words and a charming smile. They watched as I rode and fired, showed them the workings of my rifle and how far it could shoot. The indunas listened when I spoke of the battles I had fought and the sights I had seen.

"If the Zulu had been at the Crater," one grizzled induna said, "we would have defeated your enemies."

I was not sure what to say to that so merely agreed.

"Are your enemies still searching for you?" the same induna asked.

"They might be," I said, cautiously.

"Will they come into Zululand for you?"

"They don't know I am here," I said.

The induna. "I will speak to the king," he said. "Nobody outside Zululand will know about you."

In Zululand, when the king gave an order, it was obeyed. I do not think that anybody outside Zululand ever knew that I was in the kingdom and that Inyathi was an ex-Buffalo soldier of the 9th US Cavalry.

In that first month, Cetswayo granted me a hut inside Ulundi, and later, when he saw that I needed more space to train his men, he allowed me a small kraal two miles from the capital. I made my home there, with my lonely hut on top of a small knoll.

During the day, I checked the firearms that the Zulus brought me and trained some men in their use. The guns were of all types and varieties. Traders from Portuguese Mozambique brought them in, as well as British and Jewish merchants. Most were of poor quality, ancient Tower Muskets that probably saw action against Bonaparte, muzzle-loading antique pieces and a few modern rifles stolen from settlers, Boers or perhaps soldiers.

I lacked the skill to repair them, so a Zulu blacksmith moved into my kraal and worked to my specifications. He brought his three wives and their children, plus their cattle, so my kraal became livelier.

"Where is your wife?" the blacksmith asked me.

"I don't have a wife," I told him.

He sighed. "A man needs at least one wife, and better with two or three."

Two days later a shy young woman appeared at the door of my hut. I greeted her with a smile and asked who she was.

"I am Zobuhle," she said. "The king sent me as your first wife if you like me."

Zobuhle was beautiful, plump, pretty and with the moon face and huge smile of the most beautiful women in Zululand, which means the most beautiful in the world. From the first, we got along well, for I have never wanted to beat women, and she organised my household with tact and skill. Her cooking was as good as any woman in Zululand, and we settled down as man and wife without any difficulties.

Unfortunately, although I hoped to improve and modernise the weaponry of the Zulus, the indunas did not trust firearms. They put their trust in the traditional methods of warfare that had stood them in good stead since the days of Chaka. That almost legendary king had ruled Zululand about fifty years before my time and changed them from a minor tribe to a major power. He had revolutionised their fighting methods. At that time the local tribes faced each other at fifty yards or so, threw a few spears and one group or other ran away. Chaka shortened the assegais to make a stabbing weapon known as the iXwa, with an 18-inch long blade on a shaft some 30 or so inches long. Armed with the iXwa, the Zulu impis surrounded the enemy and massacred them all.

Such ruthlessness had been unknown, and as Chaka conquered his neighbours, he had assimilated the survivors into his kingdom until he had a Zulu empire. At the time I arrived, in 1878, Cetswayo had an army some 50,000 strong, which meant in manpower it was larger than the US Army or anything the British or Boers had in Southern Africa. That figure included impis of men in their sixties and seventies, so the real fighting strength was probably about 40,000.

The weakness of the Zulus was their failure to adapt to more modern weapons. They relied on the stabbing iXwa, with an oval cowhide shield. The warriors used the shields as a weapon, distracting the enemy while they thrust upwards with the iXwa. There was also the knobkerrie, a long stick with a knob-like end that the warriors used to brain their enemies.

To use these weapons, the Zulus had to come to close quarters. They could run 40 to 50 miles a day, and fought in a manner Chaka taught them. They formed a semi-circle, facing their enemy, with the central section known as the chest of the bull and each flank the horns. Behind the chest was a reserve, the loins. They approached the enemy at a run, surrounded them with the horns and closed for the kill. They were efficient, brave, well-disciplined and deadly.

The weaknesses are evident. They had few firearms, no cavalry and no artillery. As individual fighting men, the Zulus were superb, but against a modern army, they were outmoded. Artillery and steady rifle fire should destroy their formation and numbers as the Frontier Police had done to the Galekas at Ibeka.

Cetswayo asked each induna to send men to me for firearm

training. They obeyed, of course, but the men were not the best quality. The indunas sent their lame, their stupid and whoever they least wanted in their impis. I did what I could with the men they sent, but most made poor marksmen. The Zulus seemed to believe that the harder they pulled the trigger, the faster the bullet would travel, and I had a tough job convincing them otherwise. I think one in ten would have been passable marksmen, with most preferring their assegais. Perhaps with more time, I could have trained the younger men in musketry, but although I did not know it, time was running out for the Zulu Empire.

I was content there, with Zobuhle all that a wife should be, an interesting occupation, a small herd of cattle and the friendship of the blacksmith and his family. I liked to sit at the gate of my kraal in the evening, watch the sun sink over the rounded hills of Zululand and hold William's pipe.

"Well, William," I said quietly. "We are home in Africa. I wish you were here with me. What stories we would tell our grandchildren, and what wonders we could reveal to their world."

Zobuhle respected my hour alone in the evening. She watched me from inside our hut, and when I returned home, she had the sleeping mat ready. She was young, and not as skilled in the arts of love as most of the women I had known, but she was energetic, enthusiastic and loyal. I soon taught her a few tricks to please us both.

It was a few months after I arrived in Zululand that I began to hear the rumours of impending trouble.

Since I arrived in southern Africa, I had heard stories about confederation. The British like things tidy, and to them, tidy means under British control. In their minds, all the British colonies should be joined together, with no inconvenient little independent nations in between. They called it a "forward policy," and I thought it meant they looked for an excuse to invade, defeat and annexe all the small countries they could. In

1877, the British annexed the Boer republics, much to the disgust of the Boers. However, one of these Boer republics, Transvaal, had a border dispute with the Zulus, so after annexation, the British inherited this trouble. Until they took over the Transvaal, the British had supported the Zulus; now that the land in question could belong to them, the British put their weight on the Boer side.

The British High Commissioner, Henry Bartle Frere, established a Border Commission to investigate the problem, or so he claimed. I think Frere wanted to seek reasons for a war with the Zulus. He must have choked on his brandy when his Border Commission found for the Zulus. I was always surprised to find fair dealing and honesty on such occasions. However, Frere was not finished yet and fixed on some minor infringements when Zulus crossed the frontier into British territory. Frere magnified petty crimes into major international incidents and ordered Cetswayo to hand over some Zulus to British justice.

The situation was simple. Two wives of a Zulu chief had taken lovers and fled into Natal. The chief sent a small impi after them, which recaptured and executed both women. Frere demanded that Cetswayo hand over the men who crossed the border and told him to disband his army.

Cetswayo naturally refused, and the British declared war. There might be other factors that I don't know about, but I was only a simple soldier and can only relate what I know.

With Cetswayo's refusal to agree to Frere's arrogant demands, he had played the British game. Frere knew he would not disband the army and now had an excuse for war. In Frere's eyes, victory was assured. March in a few battalions of British infantry, let the Zulus attack and blast the spear-carrying hordes with artillery and volleys from massed Martini-Henry rifles. It should all have been so simple, but the British forgot two things. One was the poor quality of British generalship, and the other was the high quality of the Zulu warriors.

The British seem to produce brave soldiers and terrible officers. As a one-time American, I heard about the Battle of New Orleans, where their general ordered them to stand in line and be slaughtered by American artillery, out of range of the British muskets. That standard of leadership seems to have continued to the present day if what I've heard is correct. The British augmented their regulars with locally raised colonial irregulars plus black infantry, known as the Natal Native Contingent. These, the NNC, were probably the lowest level of soldiers in Africa, being poorly armed, terribly officered and terrified of the Zulus. Their uniform was no more than a red rag tied around the forehead, and their weapons were spears and a handful of obsolete guns. Augmenting these men was the Natal Native Horse, who were mainly Basutos riflemen, an altogether more effective fighting unit.

I expected the call to Cetswayo and answered at once.

"We are at war, Inyathi," he said simply.

"Yes, Your Majesty," I agreed.

"I will send riflemen to you," the king said. "Await my orders."

"Yes, Your Majesty."

I was a soldier. Cetswayo had welcomed me into his country, and I would fight for him as hard as I fought for the United States or the Frontier Police. I had no problems with loyalty, or of switching my allegiance to fight the British. The thought never entered my head.

I FIGHT THE BRITISH

*T*he British invaded Zululand in three columns. I rode
out with my twenty riflemen to watch what the British
called the No 3 or Central Column. It was the 11th January 1879,
early in the morning, with mist and rain drenching us as the
British crossed the Buffalo River.

"My river," I said, watching the British set up a battery of
artillery to cover the crossing. They sent over a troop of mounted
NNC first, with the current sweeping half-a-dozen away, so their
drowned bodies bobbed and tossed downstream. Nobody made
any attempt to save them.

"All the less for us to kill," one of my men said.

When the NNC horsemen rode on patrols on our side of the
Buffalo, a red-coated British infantry regiment crossed on flat-
bottomed punts. I watched them, recognising the 24th Foot,
veterans of the war against the Galekas. They arrived on Zulu
soil, spread out in extended order and guarded the bridgehead
while the remainder of the column crossed, men, horses and a
host of supply waggons.

"We should fire on them," my riflemen said.

I was tempted, but with limited ammunition and hundreds
of horsemen opposing us, I think our intervention would only

have led to an early death. Instead, I sent a man back to Cetswayo with news of the invasion and observed the British. They moved slowly, consolidating their position before attacking the nearest kraal, the home of Sihayo, the man whose wives had absconded.

The British pushed the NNC into the attack, and this time I led my riflemen forward. We were too few to make much difference but joined the local men. The kraal was in a gorge with a rocky hill behind and, as I expected, my riflemen were too eager and opened fire too early.

"By whose orders do you invade the land of the Zulus?" I shouted.

"By the orders of the Great White Queen," somebody replied, and the NNC, with some Zulu allies, advanced.

We opened fire again, and Sihayo's men rolled down a few rocks. The NNC turned to run, only to find the 24th Foot behind with levelled bayonets, and they decided Sihayo's Zulus were less formidable and returned to the fight. I shot one of the British Zulus, and then Sihayo's followers fled.

That skirmish opened the fighting in the Zulu-British War of 1879. We watched the invaders work on the road into Zululand, then inch their waggons forward, mile by mile. After a few days, the column had creaked ten miles, to camp beneath a rocky hill known as Isandhlwana. The mountain is an isolated extension of a spur of the Nqutu Platea, the edge of which forms an escarpment. We watched as the British set up a sprawling camp, with the red tunics of the 24th Foot like specks of blood on the brown surface of Africa. In front of them was open ground, excellent territory for a Zulu army to form, but a killing ground for the massed rifles of the 24th. Their rear was vulnerable, I thought and reported as much to Ntshingwayo kaMahole and Mavumengwana kaMdlela Ntuli, the indunas who commanded the main Zulu army.

I expected the British to draw their waggons into a circle, a laager, as the South Africans termed the formation. When the

British failed to laager, I sent another message to the main Zulu army. The next day, the British commander sent away a sizeable portion of his command to the south-east. My riflemen waited, unobserved by the British pickets as the redcoats drifted around their open camp and the NNC did nothing at all. The following morning the British general Chelmsford left the camp with another large force. Three hours later, the Zulus struck.

Ntshingwayo kaMahole and Mavumengwana kaMdlela Ntuli came from the north, across the plateau and along the spur towards the British camp. They also struck from the east. The indunas had not intended to attack until the following day, but a British patrol stumbled upon the 20,000 strong Zulu army on the plateau. As soon as they saw the British horseman, the Zulus knew they must fight. They rose together, the unCijo, the umHlanga and the uThulwane, with the Nokene and Nodwengu on the right and the inGobamakhosi and umBonambi on the left. Also on the left was the uVe, who I had seen at Ulundi.

Sitting on the escarpment with my riflemen, I was thrilled at the sight. I watched this powerful African army, advancing in their unique style, with native weapons against the men who had invaded their – our – country. Whatever I write about the British politicians, I cannot deny the bravery and fighting ability of the British soldier, the red-coated privates and NCOs. They held the spur as long as they could, firing disciplined, aimed volleys that killed scores of Zulu warriors.

They withdrew, still fighting, down to the main camp. My men and I, secure on the spur, fired at them, killing a few as they faced the regiments to their front. As the Zulus pressed down the spur, another force advanced from the east to outflank the British. A third was on the west. It was the classic Zulu chest-and-horns formation.

I am still not sure what happened next. The British were fighting well, with disciplined firepower mowing down the Zulus, and then in some areas, the firing faltered. Perhaps they ran out of ammunition. I heard a story that the NNC, poorly armed and officered, broke and ran, and that may be true. I saw the Zulu army sweep around the red coats, and I heard a British bugle shrilling retire. I saw the NNC trickle away, running before the Zulu advance, with many of the camp followers among them, and then the civilian volunteers. I did not see a single red-coated soldier try to flee. They died in line when the Zulu horns closed behind them; they died in the camp, fighting back to back with their bayonets against ten times their number of Zulus, or they died among the rocks, fighting to the end. I saw one group firing until they had no ammunition, then charged the Zulu army with their bayonets fixed.

Bayete, 24th Foot. We won the battle, but you died like men.

After the victory, the Zulus stripped the dead and ripped open their stomachs to allow their souls to escape. We took the arms and ammunition and looted the camp, leaving nothing we thought valuable. It was a gruesome sight, hundreds of naked dead men, and we had suffered too. I heard there were about 2000 Zulu dead, and hundreds more wounded.

After that victory, many Zulus celebrated, thinking they had defeated the British invasion. "No," I told Ntshingwayo kaMahole, "that is not how the British fight. They will be hurting at the defeat and will want vengeance."

I was right, of course. After the two battles of Isandhlwana and Rorkes Drift, there was elation in Zululand, quickly followed by mourning as the war ran its course and the extent of the Zulu losses became apparent. While the British fought off a Zulu attack at Rorkes Drift, the other two British columns won their battles, dug into fortifications and waited for reinforcements. I returned to my kraal and Zobuhle and took no part in the subsequent actions until the very end of the war. I checked over many of the captured Martini-Henry rifles, kept one for my own use, made love with Zobuhle and listened to the news that men brought me.

It was mostly bad. We won a small battle at Intombe, and another at Hlobane, and that ended the Zulu victories. The

British won a major victory at Kambula, and another at Gingindhlovu, after which a second, and more extensive British invasion took place. The king, aware of the enormous casualties his people had already suffered, tried to negotiate a peace deal. When the British refused, I knew that Zululand was doomed. I had been at home here, so when the king called up the survivors of his shattered regiments to fight, I rode to join them with my few mounted riflemen.

I found the mood of the indunas sombre. They knew their tactics were outmoded and the British rifles outmatched their spears. All the same, they saluted Cetswayo with a resounding Bayete as they trotted to their final fight against the invader. I rode alongside them, proud to be in the company of such brave men. At that time, I was Inyathi of the Zulus, and at home.

The British invasion proceeded steadily, with more men than before, and defensive precautions taken with each camp. The British had learned the lesson of Isandhlwana; they did not underestimate the fighting prowess of the Zulus. The king tried to negotiate again, but Chelmsford, the general who had lost at Isandhlwana, demanded the surrender of an entire Zulu regiment. Nobody expected that to happen. The British advanced in the form of a gigantic square and halted within sight of Ulundi.

"Here we go," I said to my riflemen. I knew we were facing defeat. All the Zulu veterans, the survivors of the previous battles, knew they were fighting for a lost cause. Still, they were Zulus, the children of heaven, a proud warrior race defending their country from invasion.

The British soldiers were mixed. Some had recently arrived, with bright scarlet uniforms. Others, the veterans, were shabby, sweat-stained, sun-browned and battered. They waited for the Zulu attack, leaning on their Martini-Henry rifles, chewing tobacco, smoking stubby pipes, hard-eyed and viciously determined to avenge Isandhlwana.

I watched them with my heart sinking. I knew what type of

men these were. I stood on a ridge, just out of rifle range as the British square – or rectangle – made its final preparations, with some of the Colonial irregular horse scouting the ground in front. I watched the Frontier Light Horse canter towards me, wondering who I was. Without waiting until they came close, I trotted away.

As the Light Horse followed me, the inGobamakhosi, about 5,000 strong, rose from the long grass and stood in full battle array, with the other regiments following their example. Even after their losses, nearly 20,000 Zulu warriors faced three sides of the British square. Some instinct made me dismount and join their ranks, still holding my rifle. At that moment, I was all Zulu. The regiments stamped their feet in unison, rattled the butts of their assegais against their cow-hide shields and chanted their war-cries, boosting their spirit for the attack on the waiting rifles of the redcoats.

The Frontier Light Horse and other irregular units approached the Zulu army, fired and withdrew, causing some casualties. I shot one man from his saddle, and the Zulu army moved forward in a slow, disciplined advance. As we closed, the British artillery opened fire, blasting holes in our ranks. Men fell, with the massive Martini-Henry bullets causing terrible wounds.

We moved faster, approaching the waiting red squares, and then the Gatling gun opened up. I had never seen one before, and its multi-barrels tore into our ranks, knocking over our men in dozens. The artillery changed to case shot that killed and maimed. Our front rank died, and men began to fall to the ground, taking cover. I knelt, firing as fast as I could, trying to kill the gunners, feeling the sweat run into my eyes. I was crying, for I knew I was seeing the death of this African kingdom that had given me a home.

The Zulu reserve, the loins, rose and charged forward, only for the Gatling and massed rifles to shoot them down. If the warriors had survived the bullet storm, they would have faced four ranks of bayonets, wielded by men with no mercy in their hearts.

As the final charge faltered, Chelmsford let loose his cavalry. The Lancers, with their badge of a skull-and-crossbones, chanted "Death! Death!" as they rode out. The Zulus fled before the stabbing lances and slicing swords. I ran as well, running for the high ground until British artillery shells began to explode around me. I changed direction, found my horse and galloped for the Mbilane River, where half a dozen of my riflemen joined me.

The lancers were coming, spearing the fleeing Zulus, killing the wounded, jabbing, again and again, still chanting "Death!"

"What will we do, Inyathi?" my riflemen asked.

"Shoot them!" I said.

We stood there at the ford of the river, firing at the lancers, emptying a saddle or two, but we were too few and they were too well trained. We delayed the British for a few moments, possibly saving the lives of some of our retreating men. Then we ran again, jinking and dodging along the banks of the Mbilane River.

The battle was lost. The kingdom was lost. I knew the British would take over, and I had no desire to remain in a conquered country. As the British horsemen ran after the fleeing Zulus, I circled and returned to my own kraal.

I had met many women in my life and liked quite a few of them, but Zobuhle was the only one I would have returned to in such a situation. The others were merely women, while Zobuhle was my wife. Until that moment, I don't think I realised the difference.

WE FLEE ZULULAND

"*W*hat's happening?" Zobuhle was calmer than I expected. "I heard the gunfire."

"The British defeated us," I said. "We're leaving."

Zobuhle made no fuss. She grabbed some necessities and followed me out of the hut. "Where are we going?"

I had the answer ready. "To the hills." I indicated the distant Drakensberg Mountains.

The blacksmith came out of his forge, with his wife and children at his side. "I'll come too," he said.

"We'll have to move fast," I said.

Leading the horse, I led my people south-west. Using my military experience, I knew where the British patrols would be and avoided them as we left Zululand, the nation that had given me my first real home. The days passed, with the smoke of burning kraals in the distance and fear in the air. We passed other refugees; warriors and small family groups. A few attached themselves to our party, so we were thirty strong when we came to the borders of Basutoland. King Letsie was the present ruler, and although the kingdom was under British protection, I knew there was no garrison.

"Will they let us settle here?" Zobuhle asked.

"We'll soon see."

I had spoken to many Basuto when I was with the Frontier Police. They had all told me about their mountainous home, where their previous king, Moshoshoe, had defeated a British army. Although it had been in my mind if the Zulus had rejected me, I had not expected to come with a band of fleeing refugees.

I did not see Letsie. He had heard of our coming and sent a body of armed horsemen to usher us away.

I rode forward to meet them.

"The king says you cannot enter his lands," the leader of the Basutos said.

"Why not? We are peaceful."

"The king will not allow any Zulus into Basutoland while the Zulus are at war with the British."

I started to protest until I noticed there were other mounted men on either flank, lithe men with rifles held ready across their laps. They would shoot down my little body of refugees.

"Come on," I said to my people. A handful more had joined us, individual warriors shocked by the carnage of Ulundi, a small Border family and three herdboys who had lost their families. I now had forty followers and nowhere to go.

We moved on, skirting the borders of Basutoland, avoiding the odd British or colonial patrol as we moved deeper into the mountains. We hunted for game, using the skills my Apache woman had taught me to catch anything edible, pushing into the ever more inaccessible countryside. We headed north, day after day, until a band of wild riders blocked our path.

I did not recognise the tribe. "Who are you? You are not Basuto."

"Letsie does not rule here." They moved into a line facing me, a dozen men, some in native clothes, others in cast-off European clothing.

"Good," I said. "We are no friends of the Basuto." Tall

mountains rose around us, with mist coiling around the peaks. To my left, I saw the silver thread of a waterfall within the green border of vegetation.

"We are no friends of anybody," the leading man said.

I frowned, trying to work out who these people were.

"Oorlam," Zobuhle said quietly, "half-Khoi, half-Boer."

I had heard of these people. The Khoi were the Hottentots, the original inhabitants of the Cape, before the Boers or the black Africans arrived. The Boers called the Oorlam the Bastaards, and the British called them Griqua, a semi-nomadic people who lived mainly in the northern Cape Colony. They were sometimes friendly, sometimes not. This splinter group were evidently not friendly.

"What do you want?" I asked.

"Everything," the Griqua spokesman said. "Everything you have, starting with your horse and your weapons."

I sensed my people tense behind me. For the first time in my life, I felt responsible for a group of humans. When I was a corporal in the 9th Cavalry, my troopers were trained soldiers, and I had been young and foolish. Now I was married, and these refugees looked to me for leadership.

"If we do that," Zobuhle said quietly, "these Oorlam will kill us all. We are Zulu."

"Usuthu!" I yelled the Zulu warcry and shot the Griqua spokesman. Even as he fell, I reloaded the Martini-Henry and shot another before they realised what was happening. The warriors behind me needed no more warning. Some had fought at Ulundi or other battles and threw themselves into an attack. I slid off my horse, pushed Zobuhle behind a rock, reloaded and lifted my rifle. Three of the Griqua were down, and one of my young herd-boys. Two of my warriors were struggling with the Griqua, lunging at them with their assegais. I aimed at the closest Griqua, fired and saw him stagger back, wounded.

"Come on, Zulus!" I shouted and charged forward, using my rifle as a club. I heard the report of a firearm and felt the hot passage of a shot close by my ear. The Griquas had not expected opposition and were pulling back, with the man I wounded staggering as he ran.

Another Griqua was on the ground, screaming as a Zulu plunged his assegai into his stomach. "Sigidi!" my Zulu shouted. "I have eaten!"

All six surviving Griqua were running, spurring their horses in their effort to get away. "Chase them," I ordered. "They might be getting help."

My men understood and ran forward, fleet-footed despite the long weeks walking since we left Zululand. I was not as fast.

"Stay here!" I shouted to the women, children and older men. "Zobuhle! Keep them out of sight!" I saw my wife raise her hand in acknowledgement and ran after my Zulus.

The Griqua were well ahead, but slowing as they followed a steep path up the side of a mountain. I caught up with my men. "Let them lead us upward," I said. "We don't know this path."

My Zulus grinned to me, happy to be warriors after so long travelling. After ten minutes or so, the Griquas halted.

"They're dismounting," I said, recognising the sounds I had heard so often before. "The path must be steeper."

I pushed in front. The path was narrow and twisting, gleaming with wet from the mist, scattered with rocks. The noises from above faded as we moved, higher and ever higher. I could hear the waterfall I had seen earlier and wondered who had made this path, and when, and why. I doubted the Griqua had the time and desire, so it must have been somebody before them, perhaps a forgotten tribe from hundreds of years ago.

I heard the crack of a rifle above and ducked, shouting to my men to do the same. The bullet smashed against a rock at my side, leaving a peculiar blue-grey smear. I can see that mark still and wonder how the Griqua marksman failed to hit me. Lying behind a group of jagged boulders, I peered upwards into the mist, searching for movement and seeing none.

"I'll go forward, Inyathi," Bafana, one of my warriors said, gripping his assegais.

"No," I shook my head. I knew the fighting qualities of my Zulus, but also knew I was more experienced in hunting the enemy in this type of terrain. "I will go. Remain here, and listen for my words."

Leaving the path for the steep mountainside with its treacherous, sliding boulders, I moved slowly, holding my rifle ready. I remembered hunting Apaches along the Texas frontier, so many years ago now, and knew these Griqua were every bit as dangerous.

I tried the old trick of throwing a stone to entice the Griqua to fire at the clatter. If they had, the muzzle flares would give away their position. I knew there were six of them, and they were familiar with this territory. They did not respond.

"Hey! Griqua!" I chanced a shout, keeping my head well down. My voice echoed, distorted in the mist. "You left half your men down there."

When there was no reply, I wondered if I should chance moving again. I was nervous that the Griqua would creep up in the mist and capture me. I loosened the knife in my belt and moved on, slowly, one step at a time as the mist clung at me with clammy fingers.

Somebody called ahead, a woman's voice, high pitched. I could not make out the words.

"Who's that?" I shouted. "I am Inyathi of the Zulus."

The voice called again, and I swear it was pleading for help.

"We're coming!" I shouted and slumped behind my rock as a volley of shots followed my words. I saw the bullets lift volcanoes of dust and rock chips and ran forward, hoping to find more cover before the Griquas reloaded. All six had fired at once, which showed poor organisation. They would have been better to have some firing and others reloading.

Timing my run, I rolled into a hollow and lay still. The mist swirled around me, a sure sign that there was wind this far up the mountain. With luck, the breeze would dissipate the haze, and I could see my enemy.

"Inyathi!" One of my Zulus shouted from below. "Are you still alive?"

If I replied, I would have given away my position. I said nothing, aimed my Martini-Henry uphill and waited for events to unfold. On the Texas frontier, one learned patience or died, yet I did not wish to worry Zobuhle. I grunted; love is a strange thing that can weaken a man.

I sensed, rather than saw, movement ahead. It was nothing, a flicker in the mist that should not be there. Without conscious thought, I aimed and fired, then rolled away to reload. The Martini-Henry has a vicious kick and needs to be controlled like a young colt or a disobedient child, yet I knew my shot had taken effect.

The Griquas fired back, with bullets crashing around me. I saw one burrow into the thin soil, raising a tunnel in the ground. How many shots? I counted them in my head as I frantically thrust a cartridge into the breech of my rifle.

Five. Five, not six. I must have hit another Griqua.

"Inyatha? Are you all right?" That same voice from below, closer now. At least one of my men was coming up the path. I knew that unless I moved, my Zulus would rush towards me and the Griquas, with the advantages of position and rifles, could kill them all. However, the Griquas knew roughly where I was. If I moved, they might kill me.

"Griquas!" I shouted. "We outnumber you, and we're all armed. If you throw down your weapons we won't hurt you!"

As I hoped, the Griqua response was a volley aimed at my voice. Rising, I ran forward, shouting the Zulu war cry. "Usuthu!"

If I reached the Griqua before they reloaded, and my Zulus took the hint, I might survive. I saw vague shapes ahead, men hurrying to load their rifles, a man staring at me, open-mouthed, another raising his weapon towards me. I shot him, as being the most immediate threat, then swung my Martini at the staring man, and missed. Somebody leapt on my back, knocking me to the ground, and I felt the keen bite of steel at my throat.

I AM HOME IN AFRICA

"*U*suthu!"

That welcome cry sounded in my ears simultaneous with a jet of hot blood as Bafana thrust his assegai into the man on my back. My Zulus were here, killing the Griqua without mercy. Within a few seconds, we were the only live men on that path, and the mist was thinning. I looked around me. We were near the summit of a flat-topped mountain, where a plateau stretched ahead of us to a small village of stone-built huts.

"They build in the Basuto style," Bafana said, wiping blood from the blade of his assegai.

I agreed. I loaded my rifle before moving into the village, with my Zulus behind me, spread out and holding their assegais ready to fight. There was no need. The only male Griqua was about six years old and crying.

"What is this place?" Bafana asked. "There are no men."

Bafana was correct. There were no men, although the village had about twenty stone huts, thatched with grass. The single woman who watched us was tall and dignified; she did not flinch from our weapons.

"Who are you?" she asked. "Where are our masters?"

"All dead," I said. "Who rules this place? Are we in the land of the Griquas? Or the land of the Basutos?"

The woman gave a little shiver. "You have killed the rulers of this mountain."

"Are you saying that there is no chief here?" I asked, looking around. "How do you live?"

The woman told me that they used to live by agriculture and raising cattle until a few years ago when the Griqua band killed the men and took over. "Now we are slaves," she said, "the Griquas rob and plunder and make us work for them."

"How many people are here?" I asked.

While we had been talking, my Zulus had been investigating the village, opening doors and hauling the inhabitants outside. They stood in a huddled group, staring at us as they wondered if we were about to kill them, or worse. None of the women was over forty, and there were no men.

Zobuhle joined us, having hurried up the path. She stepped to my side, where she belonged.

"This is a village of slaves." I recognised the cowed attitude of the people. "Did the Basuto king not come to help you?"

I learned that we were outside Basuto territory. Neither Boer, Basuto, nor any other tribal group claimed this area of wild land.

"You said you used to rear cattle," I said. "Where are they now? Where did they pasture? This land is too barren."

All my followers had struggled up the path, with my herd boys running around, exploring everything as Zobuhle examined the huts with a critical eye.

"Down here, Inyathi," one of the herd boys shouted, waving to me with a broad grin on his face. I hurried to him, on the other side of the village. A path led downwards to a shallow valley, facing the sun, and fertile with grass. A score of cattle grazed contentedly, ignoring us.

"We have cattle," Bafana said.

"We have cattle," I agreed.

"This is our home now," Zobuhle announced solemnly.

"When we're home in Africa," I said, touching William's pipe. I sensed him at my side, nodding in approval. We were home in Africa.

We settled there, with my refugees merging with the original population. They came from a variety of tribes, some Sotho like the Basuto, other survivors who had made their way to this remote spot after surviving tribal wars and massacres on the High Veldt. I did not care where they were from, as long as they remained with us.

We rebuilt the houses, with Zobuhle taking her place as the head woman of the village. I did not ask to become chief, but the others treated me as such, so I assumed the position with as good a grace as I could.

The situation of our village was good, with the mist and rain providing excellent water, the hidden valley providing pasture for our cattle, and the inaccessibility a measure of security from any possible aggressors. We collected the rifles and ammunition from the Griquas, in case of need, and settled down. Zulus are a self-sufficient people, and I had no desire to go elsewhere. I had my freedom, my wife and my home and want nothing else. In time we produced children, and Zobuhle demanded that I take other wives to help her, which I did.

The little herd-boy found the ancient paintings in a cave on our rocky plateau, and Zobuhle and I admired them. We often wondered who had made them and never agreed. It must have been some other tribe, maybe hundreds of years ago. We spent many hours in that cave, talking and in other pursuits, and I could feel the presence of the artist. I am sure William was there too, smiling, happy to be home in Africa.

It was years later that the British patrol came riding past our home. I always had boys on watch in case of predators, so I had warning of the British approach. A few travellers had walked or ridden past, but none had found the hidden track until this inquisitive British officer looked upwards. As bad luck would have it, there was no mist that day, which encouraged the officer in command to dismount from the horse and climb the path.

"Shall I kill him, Inyathi?" Bafana asked, cradling his assegai with the old fire in his eyes.

"No," I said. "He is alone. If we kill a British officer, the British will send a punitive expedition with great guns and destroy us." I did not admit how sick I felt at the sight of that officer, knowing what he represented.

When the officer reached the top, he removed his pith helmet and looked about him. Two of my warriors were watching, Bafana with his assegais and Bangizwe, my one-time herd-boy, with a Martini-Henry rifle. I walked towards the intruder.

"Good lord!" the officer wore the insignia of a colonel and had the lines of maturity on his face, although his eyes were as bright as I remembered, and the voice as youthful. "Is that you, Buffalo Soldier?"

I greeted Weston solemnly, not sure what he would do. If he tried to arrest me for horse stealing or desertion, I would kill him and lead my tribe onwards to fresh pastures.

"It is me, Colonel Weston," I said.

"Jolly good," Weston said. "I must say I'm glad to see you. One never knows what sort of scoundrel one will run into in these hills. It's good to meet an old comrade and friend." When he held out his hand, I knew I was safe. When a gentleman of Weston's type offers his hand, he is not going to betray you.

"It's good to see you too, Colonel. I can offer you what hospitality I can."

"Is the chief of this place around?" Weston asked. "I am afraid I must talk to him."

"I am the ruler," I said, waving away Bafana and Bangizwe.

"Well, you've done well for yourself," Weston said. He lifted his hat politely to Zobuhle.

We spoke inside my house with Zobuhle listening, and my people gathered outside.

"You see," Weston said, holding his hat in his hands. "There's been a spot of bother in Basutoland, and we're trying to round up all the malcontents."

I nodded. "We are not in Basutoland," I said.

"So, who is your overlord, your king?" Weston asked.

"I have none," I said. "Except her." I nodded towards Zobuhle.

I wondered for a moment what Weston would say. He smiled. "You are your own man then, Inyathi," he said. "You are probably the most free man I have ever met." He smiled. "I won't tell anybody of your presence here, Inyathi. I owe you that for saving my horse."

He returned down the mountain, and I never saw him again. Colonel Weston kept his word, and from that day to this, no British soldier or settler, and no Boer, has come to our village high in the Drakensberg Mountains or uKhahlamba, as the Zulus call them, the barrier of spears.

I am an old man now, and often tell the tales of my youth to my grandchildren and great-grandchildren, who cluster around my feet. It was Zobuhle, my wife for the past fifty years and more, who suggested that I write down my story, in case some future generation might be interested in the tale of a wandering Buffalo Soldier. She is watching me now, still with that same broad smile on her round face, as I sit here, the aged chief of my kraal, free of any man, and with a community of free people here, home in Africa.

Inyathi

EPILOGUE

*I*t took me quite a while to read that story, and when I finished, I knew I had to find the village of which my distant ancestor spoke. When I finished, I felt proud that I had an ancestor who had struggled against such adversary. I thought that others should also read how a man could travel from slavery in the Deep South of the United States to Africa, reversing the journey that his ancestors had made.

I had no money and few possessions, but neither had Inyathi when he made his epic journeys from a slave plantation through Texas and across half the world to Africa.

Leaving my distant ancestor's possessions with a trusted friend, I took the pipe, William's pipe, and hiked and hitched across the country. South Africa is not as dangerous now as it was in Inyathi's day, but instead of British patrols, Boer burghers and tribal wars, we have muggers and gangs who are just as likely to murder a lone traveller.

Using the scant clues my ancestor left, I followed the trail through Lesotho and deep into the Drakensberg, to the border of Lesotho and South Africa. After many false starts and dead-ends, I saw an overgrown track leading up a mist-shrouded mountain, with a waterfall descending from the heights above.

I took the path, remembering the old days of a hundred years and more ago when Inyathi dared all to lead his people to safety. I could imagine the desperate scenes as I climbed the steep path, with the mist clinging to me, and I searched the rocks for the blue smear of lead bullets, without success.

When I came to the top, I gasped, for the village was still there, a small group of stone-built cottages, roofed with thatch, neatly grouped on the summit plateau.

A woman stared at me when I stood there.

"Who are you?" she asked. "I know you, yet you are a stranger."

"I am looking for the grave of Inyathi," I said.

The woman looked at me with a half-smile. "This way," she said and led me to a small mound, surmounted by an umlahlahkosi tree – buffalo-thorn tree, the tree whose name means "which buries the chief."

"That's where we buried him," the woman told me. "Who are you?"

"Inyanthi was my ancestor," I said. I knelt at the base of the tree.

"Then you are at home here," the woman said.

I looked at her. "Yes," I said. "I have come home."

I am still here.

Themba Umbalisi, RSA October 2020

Dear reader,

We hope you enjoyed reading *When We're Home in Africa*. Please take a moment to leave a review, even if it's a short one. Your opinion is important to us.

Discover more books by Themba Umbalisi at https://www. nextchapter.pub/authors/malcolm-archibald

Want to know when one of our books is free or discounted? Join the newsletter at http://eepurl.com/bqqB3H

Best regards,

Themba Umbalisi and the Next Chapter Team

When We're Home In Africa
ISBN: 978-4-86747-380-1

Published by
Next Chapter
1-60-20 Minami-Otsuka
170-0005 Toshima-Ku, Tokyo
+818035793528

19th May 2021